ABNER'S STORY

A Novel

Michael J. Bellito

Strategic Book Publishing and Rights Co.

Strategic Book Publishing and Rights Co., LLC
USA | Singapore
www.sbpra.net

For information about special discounts for bulk purchases, please contact Strategic Book Publishing and Rights Co. Special Sales, at bookorder@sbpra.net.

ISBN: 978-1-950860-40-1

Book Design: Suzanne Kelly

To my grandchildren,
Luke, Ryan, Charlotte, Andrew, and Milo,
whose young lives are a constant source of joy.

Special thanks to:

Erin Brooks,
for reading this manuscript and
discovering multiple errors along the way.

Billie Johnson,
who had the foresight to publish *Abner's Story*.
May you rest in peace.

CHAPTER 1

It was the ultimate "Cubbie occurrence." More so than Hack Wilson losing two fly balls in the sun in the critical fourth game of the '29 series; more so than the black cat circling Ron Santo at Shea Stadium in '69—as if the goat curse wasn't bad enough; more so than Leon Durham imitating a croquet wicket in the San Diego infield in '84; more so than Steve Bartman playing keep away from Moises Alou, or Alex "Iron Glove" Gonzalez booting the double-play ball moments later in 2003. Heck, it was even more bizarre than Jose Cardenal getting his eyelashes stuck or suffering sleepless nights due to noisy crickets as excuses for not playing. Or Steve Trout injuring himself by falling off his exercise bike. Or Brock for Broglio.

Believe it or not, this is what happened. The Chicago Cubs charter plane, bound for an exhibition game in Puerto Rico to conclude spring training of 2020, simply vanished while passing through the Bermuda Triangle. Disappeared. Swallowed up. Gone. The last time the world was so interested in this infamous area of ocean was when Flight 19, a squadron of WWII bombers, went missing there without a credible explanation. Ironically, that event took place in 1945, the last time the Cubs played in a World Series. During the match-up with the Tigers, Billy Sianis' goat was denied access to Wrigley Field because he smelled bad, thus beginning the longest and most tenacious curse in the history of sports.

It was a shame. 2020 was supposed to be a better year for the beleaguered team. After a series of so-so seasons that featured the usual amount of bad luck, bad injuries, and just plain old bad play, the Cubs had been picked to win their division for the first time since the 97-win season of 2008, when they repeated their 2007 failure by exiting the playoffs without a single win.

1

Some good draft picks had suddenly turned to gold, and a few overpriced free agents had actually hit well during the spring. The starting pitching looked outstanding, the relievers were reliable, and the lineup featured a lethal combination of speed and power. Yes, thought optimistic fans and sportswriters, this year could finally be the proverbial "next year."

Just before the team boarded the ill-fated flight, manager Ozzie Guillen spoke eloquently about his team's chances to reach the World Series and finally win it all, but no one could understand what he was saying. In the aftermath of the plane's disappearance, seventy something baby boomers, looking for clues, played the audio of Ozzie's remarks backwards and insisted that it said, "I saw a goat in a coat with a remote get on the plane. Surely we will not survive to come back alive." However, since it sounded pretty much the same when played forward, no one except Geraldo paid much attention to the conspiracy theories.

****

Opening day. Wrigley Field draped not in the usual red, white, and blue, but rather black bunting, a somber reminder to a stricken Cub Nation that there would be no ball game today. No peanuts, no Cracker Jack. No hot dogs or beer. In fact, there would be no game in any baseball city. Not in New York or Boston; not in Pittsburgh, Detroit, or Cleveland—cities where it was too cold to play baseball on April 1st anyway. Not even in sunny San Francisco or balmy Los Angeles.

Baseball Commissioner George W. Bush had postponed the first three weeks of the season, pushing the World Series back to the week preceding Thanksgiving. The first reason for this had nothing to do with the possibility of finding weapons of mass destruction in the cavernous bowels of Wrigley Field as his longtime critics rudely suggested. It was simply a designated period of mourning. The second reason was to allow time for an expansion-like draft to be held, giving the Cubs' brass a little time to pick young or old "unprotected" players from the other teams. Since each MLB team could protect thirty players, this left slim pickings for the "new" Cubs.

The good news: for the first time since the National League was formed in 1876 and played its opening games a few weeks *before* Custer's Last Stand, the Cubs would have a chance to start fresh. Many fans wondered if they would go so far as to choose a new nickname for the team, at once casting off the curse of the "Cubbies," a legacy of frustration and unfulfilled expectations. At the start, they had been the White Stockings, later the Colts and the Orphans. Finally, around 1900, they were given the name Cubs in honor of all their good young players. So why not have a "name that team" contest?

The venerable *Chicago Tribune* encouraged fans to do just that, and the idea spread like the Great Chicago Fire. The newspaper was peppered with possible monikers, most of them related to the city and its colorful history. Popular suggestions were the Chicago Capones, the Racketeers, or the Machine. Others campaigned for more contemporary nicknames, such as the Chicago Rahmfathers. But the favorite was the White Stockings, a return to their roots. After all, the nineteenth century had been the N.L. franchise's most successful, a period that produced *six* championships. Plus, the reclaiming of their original name would annoy current White Sox fans, causing them to whine even more than usual about North Side favoritism: "Can you believe it? They already have the best ballpark. Now they've stolen our name." But in the end, they remained the Cubs.

The draft was held on April 10th. Talk about building a new tradition. The head honchos—general manager Joe Girardi and newly named manager Ryne Sandberg—decided they would draft no worn, tired veterans whose careers were played out. Instead, they would go with a youth movement, raw talent that Sandberg could, given time, mold into dedicated players who cared more about the name on the front of the uniform than the one on the back.

Their choice of pitchers looked especially impressive. There was the tall Texan with the 100 miles per hour fastball, "Rusty"

Wood, tabbed to be the ace of the staff. Slated for the No. 2 spot was "Jolly" Jenkins, an amiable Canadian with a wicked slider and a knee-buckling curve. There was even a kid from the Boston organization who had been taught the knuckleball by former legend Tim Wakefield. The minor leaguer was forced to learn the unusual pitch when his right hand was badly twisted in a candy machine while reaching for a hanging Baby Ruth bar. The freak accident caused a permanent deformity of his fingers, which prevented him from gripping a baseball in a normal fashion. He answered to "Knuckles" Brown.

The team's new closer, "Sober" Sutter, had no such issues holding onto the baseball in preparation for his "out" pitch, a devastating split-finger fastball. He was christened by minor league teammates who never saw him take a drink of anything stronger than Mountain Dew. "Sober" said it kept him awake in the bullpen during long games.

The catcher, plucked from the Cardinal organization, was "Squats" Hartnett, the bearer of the most unoriginal nickname in the long history of the game, unless you count Lefty Grove, Lefty Gomez, and just about every other left-handed pitcher during baseball's glory years.

Speed up the middle and power at the corners was the goal when the draft began. The result: "Boom-Boom" Banks and "Hammering" Hack at first and third respectively, two sluggers about whom it was said, if they could just cut down on their strikeouts . . .

The shortstop and projected leadoff hitter was Marco Castro, supposedly a distant relative of the late Fidel. He was raw, just off the dirt diamonds of Cuba. But he had the blinding speed of the Road Runner. Thus, his nickname: "Beep-Beep." The new second baseman, "Hands" Herman, was an excellent fielder with very good bat control. He would most likely hit second, where the hit-and-run could be used like Kessinger and Beckert once wielded it.

Several outfielders were chosen from other teams. No one knew for sure who would start, but in all likelihood it would be—from left to right—"Stretch" Williams, "Shorty" Wilson, and "Chubby" Cuyler.

The nicknames of the "new" Cubs were not about to inspire a sudden outburst of optimism in the fans. Their surnames, however, might have been a bit more encouraging had the mourners given pause to consider them. But, as likely as not, the strange coincidence would have just been written off as yet another "Cubbie occurrence."

★★★★★★★★★★★★★★★★

One fan *did* consider the oddity of names like Brown, Harnett, Hack, and Williams appearing at such an opportune time. But his mind was sharper than most. His body, too, was in remarkably good shape, considering his unique circumstances. An ardent Cubs fan, he had been following the team since his childhood. And at times, he had vivid flashbacks of those back-to-back championships in 1907 and 1908. That made him the only living human being with firsthand knowledge of those eventful years. His name was Abner Doubleday Tripplehorn, and he was one hundred nineteen years old.

Perhaps not surprisingly, he seemed to be the only Chicagoan who hadn't expressed shock when the plane went missing. These were, after all, the Cubs. And as a (very) long-suffering fan, he knew what the odds were against anything going the way it was planned. He half expected to see the plane show up any day now, greeted with the next day's headline: CUBS BACK IN TOWN! OZZIE EXPLAINS MYSTERIOUS ABSENCE! Yeah, the old-timer thought, probably more hi-jinx from Ozzie's nephew Oney. So, what's the big deal? I mean, for cryin' out loud, didn't Lou Pinella get lost once driving from Chicago to Cincinnati and end up in Pennsylvania?

Still, it was a brainteaser. Where *had* the plane gone? Abner pondered this over his usual breakfast of scrambled eggs, bacon, and toast with raspberry jam. He sat in his normal spot by the window overlooking the parking lot. He had been here at the home since his early nineties. After his beloved wife Vera had passed from pneumonia at the age of eighty-nine, Abner found it difficult to keep up their neat apartment in Evanston,

5

just north of the city, and therefore decided to move into the then-new nursing home just a few blocks away. With the baby boomers approaching their final phase of life, these state-of-the-art "senior living facilities" were popping up like Walgreens on every corner.

"Senior," however, was a label he could live without. Old age, he had decided years ago, was just a state of mind. Besides, he reflected, in today's mixed-up world, one became a senior at age sixty. That meant that Abner had been a senior for half his life. Half. And since he knew he could beat the suspenders off of any sixty-year-old wannabe in checkers, chess, scrabble, and maybe horseshoes, he thought he should be treated with a little more respect.

He polished off his third piece of bacon and smiled. The doctors who looked after him were always telling him to lay off the foods that were high in fat, sodium, and cholesterol, but he paid them no mind and ate what he wanted. After his bi-monthly check-up, when his numbers showed up in the normal range and his heart continued to beat strong and true, he would always say to the perplexed physicians, "You wanna come over for lunch today? It's Tostada Tuesday. Meat, cheese, lettuce, tomatoes, olives, sour cream—we can load those suckers up. Oh, and there's an all-you-can-eat ice cream bar for dessert."

Overall, Abner was happy—spilling over with life, some might have said. The knee and hip replacements he had had in his eighties still allowed him to move around without a wheelchair, although he almost always used a walking cane for balance. He had a comfortable, clean room, which had recently become a single when his roommate had suffered a sudden—and fatal—heart attack while exercising with one of the young nurses in the swimming pool. And although Abner felt bad that the man had died, he was glad to have the room, with its flowered wallpaper and 27-inch television set, all to himself. Now he could watch "Baseball Tonight" on ESPN instead of his former roommate's preference, "Bad Girls Club."

When he finished his last bite of toast and drank his last swallow of black coffee, he slowly rose from the table, grabbed his cane, and ambled out of the dining room. Maggie, his favorite cafeteria worker, yelled after him, "Hey, Abner, you forgot to put your tray away!" It was at times like these that Abner had selective hearing, although his was as good as the average sixty-year-old.

He continued down the hallway past the nurses' station—the overworked and underpaid staff scrambling to deliver the right medicine to the right patients at the right time—and headed to his room. (They wouldn't be visiting Abner because he took no medication.) It was Room 101, the first door at the end of the hall, right next to the exit that opened onto the patio with its wrought-iron furniture and lush gardens. Even now, in early April, the tulips were beginning to push their way up out of the moist ground.

Abner entered his room and turned left into his private bathroom. He stood for a moment in front of the mirror. The glass reflected the face of a man who, all things considered, didn't look a day over ninety-nine. Rugged, chiseled features topped with silver strands of hair. A thick mustache. Vera had once told him when they were young, "Kissing a man without a mustache is like eating an egg without salt." He never liked hard-boiled eggs, with or without salt, but he kept the mustache all those years because she liked it, and that was a good enough reason for him. Over the years, it had become part of his personality, like the ever-present cigar he smoked all of his life. (He had quit cold turkey just after his seventieth birthday when his best friend had died from emphysema.) The glasses were a necessity, but Abner felt they blended nicely with his features, and they were neither too thick nor too large like Harry Caray's had been.

After he brushed his teeth—the implants were great—he headed off in the direction of the library. He had been reading a humorous fictionalized memoir by some baby boomer who had grown up in the suburbs during the fifties, and he wanted to see what happened next. But he was also hankering for a good game of checkers. Maybe Ralph or Ed would be there. Then he could punish one or the other. He admitted to himself that they were probably tired of being beaten. They also didn't like how he'd jabber throughout the game—mostly about baseball—to throw them off. And they especially didn't like the way he'd finish them off. After he set them up, he'd grin widely, reach down with a grizzled hand, and "click," "click," "click." He would then look up at his defeated opponent and say, "Quick, huh? Just like Tinker to Evers to Chance," reciting the names of the most famous double-play combo in Cubs history. But as Abner himself would readily admit, that was a *long* time ago.

CHAPTER 2

Matthew Holmes and Jason Doyle had hung out together since kindergarten. They'd met the very first day on the crowded school bus when they'd found empty seats across the aisle from each other. Because their seatmates were girls—a disorienting situation back then—they'd turned away from the cooties and into the aisle, perhaps a preordained meeting. Matt broke the ice by pulling a prized possession from his backpack and showing it to Jason. It was a 2011 Topps baseball card of Cubs third baseman Aramis Ramirez. The piece of cardboard made an immediate impression on Jason, who promised to bring a few of his own cards the next day. The boys ended up in the same classroom, and by the end of that first year together, they were fast friends.

It was, in some ways, an odd friendship. Their personalities were quite different. Matt, although certainly not shy, was quiet and thoughtful, whereas Jason was garrulous and funny. And yet Matt was clearly the leader. He most often initiated their activities, whether it was a sleepover, a bike ride, or a trip to the movies or the ballpark. Catching the El at Howard Street and taking the red line to Wrigley Field was their favorite summer pastime.

For several years now, they had managed to secure occasional tickets to the bleachers, where they would gaze down on the sun-drenched grass amid the smell of beer and suntan lotion, listening to the familiar baseball sounds that had worked their way into the fabric of their childhoods: the solid crack of the wooden bat when a power hitter made good contact; the rise and fall of the vendors hawking their peanuts and red hots; the endless taunting by the loudmouthed drunks of the opposition's outfielders, mostly in regard to the players' on-the-road relationships with various baseball Annies.

For it was the fortunes and failures of the Chicago Cubs that bonded the boys' long-time friendship more than anything else. They were too young to remember 2008, the last time the Cubs had made the playoffs. But they—like most youngsters—were hooked on hope, visualizing an N.L. pennant and World Series victory any year now. That fantasy had, of course, dissolved along with the missing plane. The familiar team that they had cheered for during the past few years was long gone, and only E.T. knew where.

Strangely, the 2020 Cubs were doing much better than anticipated. "Rusty" Wood topped the league in victories, and "Boom-Boom" Banks led in home runs and RBIs. Even more impressive than being able to boast of a few statistical leaders, the entire team was playing together like a . . . well, like a team. "Beep-Beep" Castro and "Hands" Herman turned out to be every bit as good at the hit-and-run as hoped for, and the outfield trio of Williams, Wilson, and Cuyler were blasting their way into the hearts of Cub Nation. Hardly anyone thought "Stretch," "Shorty," and "Chubby" were appropriate nicknames for them anymore, but baseball superstition wouldn't allow for a change, just as catcher Randy Hundley had refused to change his "lucky" underwear during the long, hot summer of '69. Anyway, it was so far, so good for the "new" Cubs.

****

Matt and Jason sat in Mrs. Hulbert's eighth-grade English class watching the clock tick down their final week of middle school. Because the school year was finally over and their baseball team was doing so well—three games above .500 and four games back of the division-leading Cardinals in early June—the two fourteen-year-olds basked in an enhanced state of serenity. Seldom did they dwell on the fact that, in a few short months, they would be forced to abandon all that they knew and enter high school. They thought only of the upcoming summer with its untapped possibilities: lying on sand-covered towels amidst bronze bodies on the beaches of Lake Michigan;

sipping on root beer shakes at Homer's while checking out the girls in the adjoining booth; following the day-to-day action of a pennant race on the North Side.

But their teacher's next words shattered any illusion of summertime bliss. "Listen up, boys and girls!"

The class, having no idea that the gates of Hell had just swung open before them, stopped chitchatting and focused on her stern countenance.

"In the past, Evanston Township High School has required incoming freshmen to prepare for the rigor of ninth-grade by reading a classic novel, such as *To Kill a Mockingbird* or *Of Mice and Men*. This year, however, the teachers have voted to abandon that practice."

The class broke into wild applause. Mrs. Hulbert, like a cat toying with a mouse before it bites off the rodent's head, waited patiently—and with increasing amusement—for the clamor to subside.

"Instead . . ." she paused, and the class slumped.

"Instead, students will work in pairs on a writing project. I have the topics here. We will have a blind draw to see who gets what, although they all look interesting to me." She smiled, Lucifer in beige. "Please take a few moments to pick your partner, and then we'll all choose our topics."

Our topics? thought Matt. That's a hoot. As if she'd be slaving away all summer too.

Jason leaned over. "I guess we'll be partners, huh?"

"Actually, I was thinking of asking Katie Kearns," said Matt.

"In your dreams. Can you believe this? There goes the summer."

"No kidding."

"All right, pay attention now!" Mrs. Hulbert's voice cut through the din. "Let's start on this side of the room. Come up here with your partner and draw your topic from this bowl."

Unlike Shirley Jackson's "The Lottery," there were no survivors. Stunned students were stoned with topics such as: "Write a five-page typed essay about the Columbian Exposition"

11

or ". . . about the possibility of a Monorail system being introduced to Chicago by 2025" or ". . . about television's role in the politics of the 1960s."

Matt reached a trembling hand into the black bowl and pulled out a folded piece of paper. He and Jason walked stiffly to their seats, not daring to look at each other. They sat down, hunched over, and slowly opened the paper as if it was a draft notice. Their topic read: "Write a five-page typed essay after interviewing an elderly person about his/her long life. Focus on the person's memories of great historical or technological events."

Jason sighed and said to Matt, "Your grandma. She's old."

"Wait. There's more." Matt read aloud, "You may *not* use a relative for this project."

"Well, that's just dandy," moaned Jason. "Where are we gonna find an old person, anyhow?"

"I don't know. We'll just have to dig one up somewhere. If we don't, we'll have an F in English before the class even starts."

****

Rows of maple trees lined the quiet street and blocked the mid-June sun from the two boys as they threw the baseball back and forth with rhythmic motions. They didn't speak. The only sound was the "thwack" of the grass-stained ball as it settled sharply into each boy's mitt. The game of catch in front of Matt's house was an established routine that was sometimes played out twice a day, once in the muggy afternoon and once again in the breezy warmth of a summer's evening. It ended only when one of the friends simply held the ball, removed his glove, and said, "Nuff." That was an unwritten code; no one ever asked for more time.

Most days, conversation would accompany the ritual. In fact, some serious thoughts about life's most significant aspects were often unveiled during the game. These discussions almost always revolved around girls they knew and wished they had the courage to date. But considering that they were too shy to even speak to these girls, the odds of actually going to a movie or out for ice cream with one of them were slim and none. So, just as they attempted to emulate their favorite players while throwing the ball, they also dreamed of what it would be like to have real-live girlfriends. Paper fantasies. And yet, who knew? High school would bring a new crop of honeys to the crowded hallways.

High school. The touchy subject. The reason why today, a week after graduation, the boys had nothing to say, allowing the perfect symmetry of their throws to hide the tangled terror of their thoughts.

Matt finally brought it up. "So, have you given any thought to the project?"

"No," said Jason, putting a little more than usual on his fastball.

"We have to start soon, you know," reminded Matt, adding even more zip to his return throw.

The ball caught Jason squarely in the palm of his glove, stinging badly. His temper flared. "Well, you're so smart. Why don't you think of someone to interview?"

The throw, fired with heated passion, wasn't even close to Matt. It sailed over his head like an errant bird, bounced once off the sidewalk and onto the parkway, and skidded along, stopping with a sudden "thump" against Mr. Manthey's recycling bin four doors down.

"Nice throw, chucklehead!"

"Give me a break! You didn't even try to catch it!"

"Whatever," pouted Matt, turning his back on his friend and reluctantly trudging down the street to retrieve the baseball.

Mr. Manthey, the neighborhood grouch, didn't like kids walking on his property, so Matt approached the ball with caution. It rested beside the green gem that was set out by the curb. As he reached down to grab it, something caught his eye. He froze. A newspaper, open to an inside page, was visible among the soup cans and pop bottles. He read the headline at the top of the page. He read it again.

Glancing nervously at the house, Matt clutched the paper and pulled it from the bin. As if stealing a precious gem, he tucked it beneath his arm and turned to flee. Without warning, a hand reached out and touched his shoulder.

"Aaaah!"

"What's going on?" asked Jason, who had come up from behind.

"Don't do that! You scared me half to death!"

"Well, what is it? What did you take?"

"Follow me. I'll show you."

The two boys sprinted back to Matt's house. Up the driveway. Through the side screen door. Up the stairs to the familiar bedroom. Matt dove onto his bed, rolled over, and was quickly besieged with a laughing fit, as if all the cares of the world had been removed from his shoulders. Jason, slightly winded, stood just inside the door and stared at his buddy in perplexed disbelief.

"Okay, Mr. Funny Man. Do you want to tell me what you're so happy about?"

"See for yourself," said Matt, holding up the newspaper with both hands.

Jason came closer. He bent over and read the headline that had so transformed Matt. It was a magical moment, almost as supernatural as the odd series of events that had preceded it.

The bold, black ink read: WORLD'S OLDEST LIVING PERSON RESIDING IN EVANSTON.

CHAPTER 3

A six-game winning streak in June was like a double-decker sugar cone. In the frigid air-conditioned shop, the ice cream sat proud and erect above the lip, inviting that first lick. As the tongue ran over the cold exterior, the burst of flavor—peach or strawberry or mint chocolate chip—stimulated the taste buds and soothed the dry mouth. Time stood still. Surely each successive lick would be as unhurried and easy as the first one. As satisfying too. But, one careless step out into the steamy summer air, and chaos erupted. The tightly bound substance, so sure of itself a short while ago, fell apart, sliding down the hand with increasing rapidity, coating the arm and the sidewalk below with wet, sticky globs. Out of control. A shattered, hopeless mess.

Abner angrily stabbed at the power button on the remote. The Cubs' six-game winning streak had evaporated like melting ice cream and quickly turned into a four-game losing streak. The bullpen had collapsed in the last three games, the final meltdown coming when "Sober" Sutter blew the save in the bottom of the ninth on two successive wild pitches. Oh, well, Abner consoled himself, it might not be the beginning of the end after all. The Cubs would catch the plane home where, at Wrigley the next night, they would surely turn it around against the cellar-dwelling Pirates.

The plane. Abner had a sudden flashback to March. (True, this wasn't much of a flashback for him. Most of them went back to the time when Teddy—or at least Franklin—Roosevelt was president.) He pondered the meaning of the lost flight, especially now that the "new" Cubs were suddenly having a bad week. Had the plane's mysterious disappearance, like a bad episode of "The Twilight Zone," cursed his beloved Cubs once again? The fans were now stuck with what—the equivalent of an expansion team? Abner knew darned well that most new teams needed five years or so before they were good enough to compete for a pennant. "Wait till next year" was all right for most of the loyalists but—let's face it—he was running out of time. If the lousy bums didn't win it this year, would he live to see 2021?

****

"Do you think he'll live long enough for us to do the interview?" a worried Jason asked. "I mean, the paper said he's one hundred nineteen. That's older than old."

The two fourteen-year-olds sat on the front steps of Matt's house and batted around the idea.

"Look," argued Matt, "we've been over this. We don't have any other choice. Besides, he's probably bored out of what's left of his mind. This will give him something to look forward to."

Jason rolled his eyes. "What if he doesn't remember what he did yesterday let alone way back in the twentieth century?"

"Allow me to repeat the obvious. We don't have any other choice."

"Okay," groused Jason, "but you're making the call."

"What time is it?" asked Matt.

Jason flipped open his cell phone. "Nine-thirty."

"You think he's up by now?"

"How should I know? Maybe he sleeps all day. If I ever get to be that old, that's what I'm going to do."

"You can sleep when you're dead. Hand me your phone."

Five minutes later, the deed was done.

"How did he sound?" asked Jason.

"Old," replied Matt. "And crabby. But he said we're welcome to visit him anytime we want to as long as we don't bother him when the Cubs are on."

"He said that? Do you think he's a die-hard?"

"Oh, I'm pretty sure of that."

****

16

The bus came to a stop, and Matt and Jason got off. They were both dressed in neat slacks and polo shirts. They had agreed that it would look bad to show up at Serenity Now Retirement Community wearing their usual summer shorts and T-shirts, although Jason's light blue polo was adorned with a Cubs logo. It was 9:50 am, ten minutes before their initial interview was to begin, when they entered the lobby.

The woman at the front desk was efficient. She had them sign in, gave them their name tags, and summoned a nurse to take them through the maze of corridors to wherever Abner was hanging out.

Abigail Sweeney, fifty-five, had been a nurse for her entire adult life. It was all she'd ever wanted to be. The only thing she hated about working in the nursing home for the past thirty years was the frequency with which the patients checked out. Death was, of course, a natural part of life, but it always hit her hard when someone she had looked after for years was suddenly not around anymore. That was one of the reasons she treasured her relationship with Abner. He was there in 1990 when she had started, and at times it seemed to her as if he would be there forever, teasing and tormenting her in the most affectionate way, cantankerous to the last. Everyone at the home called her Abigail or Abby; he just called her "Abs."

"He's sitting out in the garden," she said as she led the boys past yet another nurse's station. "It's such a beautiful day, and he likes to sit out whenever he can."

Pushing open a glass door, she steered them down a brick pathway lined with lush flower gardens. It was a serene setting, and it was not surprising to see a number of seniors soaking up the sun. In a clearing up ahead, the boys saw the old man sitting on a wrought-iron bench, one knee casually draped over the other, his cane tucked over his elbow. He was staring blankly out into space, and the boys wondered how much he'd be able to remember about the "good old days."

Sensing their concern, Abby smiled over her shoulder. "Don't worry. His mind is as sharp as a tack. He never forgets a thing, especially baseball statistics."

Abner shifted his gaze toward the approaching threesome. A scowl crept over his face. "Well, what have we got here, Abs? The Boy Scouts?"

"Be nice, Abner," she cautioned. "These are the young men from the high school who have come to ask you questions about your life."

"Ha!" he snorted. "What life? Why, they won't even let you have a sip of Jack Daniels once in awhile. Or invite a lady friend to your room."

Abby shook her head from side to side. "Warden's rules. Now, are you going to say hello?"

Abner looked directly into Matt's eyes. He extended his hand. "Hello."

Matt stepped forward and, afraid of what a firm shake might do, barely gripped the boney hand. "Hello, Mr. Tripplehorn. My name is Matt."

"Matt, is it? Well, Matt, you have the handshake of an infant. For Pete's sake, don't be afraid to let the other guy know you're alive." With that, Abner closed his weathered, knuckly hand around the boy's and tightened his grip. He squeezed briefly and let go. "That's how men shake hands. Got it?"

"Yes, Mr. Tripplehorn."

"And for cryin' out loud, call me Abner. If we're gonna chat, we might as well be on a first-name basis."

"Yes, sir. . . I mean Abner."

Jason stepped forward next. "My name is Jason. It's a pleasure to meet you."

They shook hands.

Abner looked at Matt. "Much better. Your friend here knows how to make a good first impression. He had more direct eye contact too. Never be timid about looking someone in the eye. That person will respect you for it."

The boys began to wonder if this was a good idea. They had been with Abner for five minutes now, and all they'd learned was a lesson in person-to-person communication. What was next? Manners?

"So, Jason, what's that you got on your shirt? It's hard to make out."

Jason leaned forward so Abner could see it better. "It's a Cubs logo, sir. We're fans."

Abner's eyes twinkled briefly. He frowned and let out a hoarse, bitter laugh. "You hear that, Abs? Looks like these fellows have a bad case of Cubs fever." He coughed and continued, "That's bad. Really bad. Why, in my life, I've seen 'em all come and go. Measles, mumps, typhoid, polio. Cubs fever is the worst. You know why? 'Cause it never gets cured. It just gnaws away at you like a diseased rat feastin' on your flesh. Why, I'd rather have shingles."

Abby laughed loudly. "Oh, Abner, stop it. You're going to make these boys think you're immune to it. But we know better, don't we? Trust me, boys, Mr. Tripplehorn cares more about the Cubs than anyone I know. Or was that Mrs. Meyer in Room 102 I heard cursing at Hartnett last week for striking out with the bases loaded?"

Abner, for once at a loss for words, crossed his arms and pouted as if deeply offended.

"I thought as much," said Abby. "Well, why don't I leave you three alone for awhile so you can get better acquainted?"

Really? thought the boys.

"I'll check back with you in a little bit." And the friendly nurse, medium to the nearly dead, was suddenly gone, leaving the terrified boys alone with Abner.

Abner looked up at Matt and Jason as if they were helpless— or hopeless. "Well, don't just stand there like a couple of Cub batters in the clutch. Pull up some chairs."

The interview went down as smooth as lemon pie. The only problem was that a suddenly amiable Abner was asking all the questions. Within forty-five minutes, the shrewd senior knew all there was to know about the teens, including their ethnic backgrounds, their high school goals, and their career aspirations. Any longer and he might have discovered their deepest fears and tightly held secrets as well.

"So, who's your favorite Cubs player?" Abner asked.

"Banks," volunteered Jason.

"I like Brown," chipped in Matt.

19

"Ah, good old 'Three-Finger,'" sighed Abner, staring wistfully out past the courtyard.

The two boys exchanged puzzled glances.

"Uh, sir," said Matt softly.

"Huh?" responded Abner, traveling quickly back through time to the moment.

"If it's all right with you, we'd like to ask you a few questions."

"Fire away."

Matt opened his notebook, produced a pen from his pants pocket, and straightened up in his chair. "What was your childhood like?"

Abner smiled. "Like no other childhood since."

Matt eagerly wrote down the quote word for word. It was a gem. A few more like this interspersed among one or two timeworn stories, and the essay would write itself.

Of course, neither boy had any idea what Abner meant by it. They could only deduce that the lifestyle he was born into at the turn of the twentieth century was so remote from any to come that it was truly unique. He was, after all, roughly the same age as the automobile. He had outgrown playing with marbles by the time the Titanic set sail. And, most significantly, he had *not* been a kid during the violence of the Roaring Twenties, the despair of the Great Depression, the horror of either World War, the madness of the sixties, or the fear of the post-9/11 decade.

But then, how grand could his childhood have been? As a boy, he hadn't known those wonderful inventions of the future: radio, television, air flight, microwave ovens, computers, cell phones, and video games. His had been a simple life.

"For example," Abner continued, "you two haven't yet experienced the joy I knew growing up when I did."

Now the boys were completely confused.

"You don't understand what I'm talking about, do you?"

Matt and Jason shook their heads slowly from side to side.

In the next few quiet seconds the old man had to decide whether it was worth it to go on. "Let me ask you a simple question. Have either of you ever heard the name Fred Merkle before?"

CHAPTER 4

Once again, Matt and Jason exchanged quizzical glances. Abner sighed wearily. "I thought as much. Fred was one of the reasons my childhood was so happy."

Matt ventured a foolish guess. "Was he the ice cream man?"

Abner's eyes crinkled at the corners. A grin crossed his lips. "Well, if by the ice cream man, you mean someone who comes along when you least expect it to brighten up an overcast day, then I guess young Fred *was* the ice cream man."

The boys' spirits sagged. Was the old man going to talk in riddles all day?

"And," Abner added, "it was his boner that gave us kids such a thrill."

That was it, thought the boys. Time to go home.

Abner stood. "Let's go inside. The sun's burnin' my brain. I'll tell you the whole story in there."

Both boys felt compelled to flee. Did they really want to record Mr. Tripplehorn's sordid stories for posterity? Or for a grade?

Matt whispered to Jason, "Remind me never to be a journalist."

"Well, are you coming or not?" Abner, several steps down the walkway, beckoned them to follow. Reluctantly, they did.

When they reached Room 101, the old gentleman gestured politely to his former roommate's bed. "Why don't you both sit there and be comfy?"

As the boys moved to the edge of the bed, Abner pulled out a desk chair, spun it around with one hand, and sat down. He rested his bony arms on the chair's back. Matt and Jason had been scared into submission, an act of willpower on their part, since the kindly figure represented not so much as a passing threat to the boys, unless it was the very real possibility of being talked to death at a young age. For, along with Abner's many formidable talents was the ability to tell stories of legendary proportions with the skill of a wizard seated beside a slowly dying fire in some medieval castle.

But before the narrative, yet another pointed question. "You boys think the Cubs suck, don't you?"

More dirty talk, thought the boys.

"Oh, I know you like 'em, and you follow 'em, and"—here he stopped and chuckled—"you actually believe they might win a championship this year. I'm not talking about that. I'm addressing the pain you feel when they always come up short or, during most years, turn out to be the doormat of the National League. You know, 'lovable losers.'"

The boys nodded in unison. It was true. It was sad. It was pathetic. The Cubs hadn't even *played* in a World Series since 1945—seventy-five years ago.

"Well," Abner said with the utmost conviction, "it wasn't always like that. Did you know that, during my childhood years, the Cubs represented the National League in *four* of the first seven World Series ever played?"

This was amazing, incredible, hard-to-believe news for the youngsters, unaccustomed as they were to anything but low batting averages, high earned run averages, and unfriendly scores more lopsided than Custer vs. Sitting Bull—or, in modern terms, Chicago vs. St. Louis.

"Or," Abner continued, "that between 1906 and 1945, a spell of forty years, they won ten N.L. pennants, an average of one every four years?"

Matt and Jason were hooked now. Their wide eyes never left the wizened figure.

"The first," Abner began, "was in 1906. I was only six, a bit young to have paid much attention. But my father sure did. As did the rest of Chicago. Wanna know why? 'Cause it was a true 'City Series.' The Cubs would be playing their cross-town rivals, the White Sox.

"Most experts figured it was over before it began. The Cubs had won 116 games and lost only 36, still the very best winning percentage in the long history of the game. The Sox were nicknamed the 'hitless wonders' on account of they had buckets of trouble scoring any runs. But somehow"—Abner paused here and released a slow sigh—"somehow the South Siders took it four games to two."

"Excuse me, sir," interjected Jason, "but isn't that just another example of the Cubs snatching defeat from the jaws of victory?"

"One might think so. But check it out on your fancy-pants Internet. Look up any list of 'Baseball's 10 Greatest Teams,' and the 1906 Cubs are on it. Remember, boys, bad things sometimes happen to great teams. The best team doesn't always win the World Series."

Matt and Jason had never considered this possibility. And yet, how could this team be considered so awesome if they never "won it all"?

"But they *did* win it all," said Abner, his mischievous grin showing that he had read the boys' thoughts. "Twice, as a matter of fact. 1907 and 1908. Beat up the Tigers both times. And the reason they could bounce back from losing to the Sox and accomplish that particular feat is on account of they had the same great players the whole time. First baseman and captain Frank Chance, second baseman Johnny Evers, shortstop Joe Tinker. And the pitching. Whoa, that was something special. Orval Overall, Ed Reulbach, Jack Pfiester, and the greatest of them all, Mordecai 'Three-Finger' Brown."

There was that name again.

"So, why was he called 'Three-Finger'?" piped up Jason.

"When he was a boy, his hand was badly mangled in a corn chopper on the family farm. It was said that the way it was all twisted up and missing a finger is what gave his curveball such a sharp break."

Matt immediately thought of his hero, "Knuckles" Brown, and the ill-fated candy machine incident that had forced the young pitcher to learn to throw his wicked knuckleball. What was going on here?

"So, anyway, when I was only eight, the Chicago Cubs were back-to-back World Series Champions." Abner stopped abruptly. His eyes were glazed over as if he was no longer there. And he wasn't. He was visiting his childhood, reliving the excitement of his boyhood idols being the best baseball team on the planet.

Matt looked down at his notebook. He hadn't written down a single word. He and his friend had been entranced by Abner's amazing tale. The boys better understood now what he had referred to as the joy he knew as a child.

"Haven't you forgotten something?" Abner was back.

"Huh?" Matt wasn't sure.

"I brought you in here to tell you a story, remember? About Fred Merkle."

The boys had been so distracted that they'd forgotten their original curiosity about the strange name.

"And no, he wasn't the ice cream man. He was a baseball player." Abner shifted in his seat. "It's nearly lunch time, and I'm hungry. So, I suggest you take notes this time, or you'll have nothing to take away with you for your report."

"Yes, sir, Mr. Abner, sir."

Abner was eating this up. For once he had an eager audience for a story he'd told a thousand times. A story that ranked as possibly the greatest moment in Cubs history.

"September 23rd, 1908," he began. "The Cubs were locked in a three-way pennant race with the Pirates and Giants, and they were playing the latter in a critical game in New York at the Polo Grounds. Score tied 1-1. Bottom of the ninth. Giants had runners on the corners with two men out."

Abner paused for effect. Jason stared wide-eyed, awaiting the outcome. Matt wrote feverishly in his journal.

The ancient storyteller wetted his lips and smiled. "To be more specific, rookie Fred Merkle standing on first base."

This was it, thought the boys.

"Base hit scored the runner from third. 2-1, Giants. Game over."

Matt stopped writing. Jason looked perplexed. Was the old man confused about the story's outcome? How could a critical loss have been good for the Cubs?

Abner laughed and clapped his hands together. "Do you see it, fellows? Can you figure out what happened next? Merkle's boner, boys. His infamous boner."

Neither boy was sure he wanted to hear more. Wasn't it lunchtime by now?

"Merkle ran off the field to celebrate with his teammates." Drool spilled over Abner's bottom lip. "He ran off the field without touching second base." His eyes were wide open. "Without touching second base. There was still a force out in play. Oh, nobody bothered with formalities in those days. Dozens of base runners regularly headed for the dugout once the winning run crossed home plate. But the baseball gods smiled down upon the Cubs that day.

"Johnny Evers called for the ball to be thrown in from the outfield. But, by now, chaos reigned. Some fans stormed the field, and one of them absconded with the ball after a Giants pitcher purposely threw it into the crowd. But Evers was no dummy. He quickly yelled for the home plate umpire to give him another one, stepped on second, and looked at the second base ump for the call."

Abner stopped talking. His breath was ragged.

"Are you all right, sir?" asked a concerned Matt.

"Fine. Fine." He inhaled deeply. "Sorry about that. Just got myself a little excited."

"The umpire called Merkle out, didn't he?" asked Jason.

"He did. Well, actually, the home plate ump, a courageous man named O'Day, made the call on account of he was the only one who'd seen Merkle fail to touch second. And because the field was now swarming with angry Giants fans, O'Day ruled that the game was a 1-1 tie and would have to be replayed at the end of the season if the two teams were tied for first."

"Which they were?" asked an incredulous Jason.

"Which they were. October 8th, 1908. Polo Grounds. Seating capacity was 35,000, but nearly three times that many showed up and tore down fences to get in. 'Three-Finger' outdueled Giants ace Christy Mathewson 4-2, and the Cubs claimed their third straight N.L. pennant. Then, they ran like rabbits for their very lives. Those crazed Giants fans threw everything at them but grandma's laundry. Bottles, rocks, you name it. Frank Chance was punched in the throat, tearing some ligaments, and pitcher Jack Pfiester's shoulder was slashed with a knife. People took their baseball more seriously back then. Anyway, the Cubs were finally escorted by New York's finest to the train station in the dead of night and made their escape. By then, they weren't too worried about the bomb threat that had been called in to the station master."

Matt and Jason felt as if they'd just climbed off a roller coaster. Did Abner really have all this baseball knowledge stored up inside his head?

"Knockin' off Detroit for the second year in a row was a piece of cake after that. The Cubs took the World Series four games to one. Have a nice day, boys."

And Abner was out the door, heading for lunch.

CHAPTER 5

The El rattled along. At ten-thirty in the morning, it carried few passengers. Matt and Jason, dressed in their Cubs jerseys and caps, stared out the dirty train windows; dirty apartment windows stared back. Suddenly, the gray-colored tombstones of Graceland Cemetery popped into view, signaling the nearness of Wrigley Field.

Graceland, eternal home to some of the most famous figures in Chicago's glamorous history, featured one baseball-shaped marker signifying the grave of William Hulbert, original owner of the Chicago White Stockings and cofounder of the National League. The baseball was etched with the names of the eight cities that comprised the N.L. in 1876. But Matt and Jason weren't interested in a worn tombstone, even if they had been aware of its existence. Their focus was on today's game. Their beloved team was hosting the New York Mets, and the boys would be looking down on the action from above. Way above. Of all the renovations—and there were many—that King Theo had ordered the crumbling edifice to undergo during his reign, one of the most exciting for fans was the addition of seats atop the old scoreboard. Theo had used the same blueprint when he'd placed seats atop the Green Monster at Fenway Park over a decade ago. Although the players looked like Munchkins from this location, the seats were sold as premium—read as expensive—seats. The boys had been fortunate to win them in a raffle at the Cubs Convention in January, and they had been eagerly anticipating the late-June Thursday afternoon game since then.

"Next stop, Addison!" crackled the train's speaker. "Addison, next stop!"

As the boys emerged from the cold shadows of the station and burst into the sunlit arena of the pre-game festivities, their hearts leapt. The colorful scene was hard to comprehend for one who was not a fan. Statues of past heroes stood silently as smiling fans, posing for pictures, clustered about them. Nearby restaurants and bars hummed with the noise of thirsty twenty somethings loudly debating the pitching match-up for the day. Scalpers slipped casually through the throng, searching for easy prey such as the middle-aged couple—day-trippers up from Peoria—or the father-son duo who had driven in from the suburbs on a whim. An unkempt vendor sold bright orange shirts with blue lettering that shouted out: The Mets Suck.

Jason laughed. "What kind of idiot would walk around wearing something like that?"

Just then, a burly man with long blond hair pushed past the boys. His orange shirt caught their eyes.

"I guess now we know," said Matt.

The ballpark's gates had been open since ten o'clock. Reversing a ridiculous policy of not letting fans in until two hours before game time, King Theo had declared: "Let them come early. Let them watch batting practice. Let them eat, drink, and get autographs. This land is their land."

And so it was.

The cavernous bowels of the ballpark greeted the boys like an old friend. Early bird specials—half-priced hot dogs and Pepsi Cola—seduced them into an eleven o'clock lunch.

"Scorecards! Get your programs and scorecards here!" barked the grizzled vendor.

"Hang on a minute. I gotta get one."

Matt loved to keep score. He had learned the art from sitting in the bleachers beside the old men who lovingly recorded every play, a virtual history that, as long as the writing never faded away, told the story of a particular game. This was in sharp contrast to many from the X, Y, and Z generations, who had no idea what the scribbled symbols meant. Nor did they care to learn. Why bother? It was tedious, time-consuming work, and one had to pay attention at all times, lest a new left fielder was inserted into the eighth inning of a tight game for defensive purposes.

But Matt understood. And a neat scorecard at game's end was something to treasure. He wondered if Abner had any old ones lying around. He would have to ask.

The boys took the elevator that had been installed behind the giant scoreboard to the gangplank that led to their seats. There had only been room to place one long row, complete with iron fences front and back, atop Wrigley's own Green Monster. It would be bad publicity indeed if a fan happened to plunge downward onto the bleacher bums below, worse even than the falling chunks of concrete that had assailed grandstand dwellers fifteen years earlier. But King Theo was not worried. He'd correctly deduced that even the most rabid of fans would not be inclined to reach out over the fences. In the first place, the odds of a hitter slamming a home run anywhere near the top of the scoreboard was astronomical, especially now that the tainted steroid era was in baseball's past. And, that temptation aside, most fans were so terrified of the height once they finally reached their seats that they remained motionless, clinging to their armrests throughout the entire game.

"Man, these are real nose-bleeders," said Jason, stating the obvious.

"Yeah," said Matt, "but look at the view. And the vendors have to walk behind us, so we can watch the game totally uninterrupted."

"True." Jason studied their surroundings. "What do we do if we have to pee?"

"Hmm. I guess we have to take the elevator back down. I'm surprised they didn't install a port-o-potty up here."

Jason laughed loudly, the wind catching the sound and carrying it behind him toward Lake Michigan. It was a hitter's wind, albeit a mild one.

Overall, the day was gorgeous. The boys found themselves perched in the middle of a cloudless sky. It was what the ballplayers called a "high" sky, the most difficult ceiling from which to catch a pop-up.

The conversation for the next two hours ebbed and flowed. There was talk of the Cubs closing in on first place—only two and a half games behind the hated Cardinals. There was talk of how the team was coming together like glue, molded by come-from-behind victories in late innings, a reliable sign of a serious contender. And there was, of course, talk of Abner.

"Amazing," remarked Jason. "I mean, he told all those stories as if they happened yesterday. How can his memory be so good?"

"I don't know," answered Matt. "What worries me is maybe he has selective memory. You know, he remembers Joe Tinker's batting average from 1908, but he can't tell you what he ate for lunch."

"Somehow I doubt that. He was pretty geared up for lunch. I didn't know someone his age could move that fast."

"Okay, I'll grant you that much—the man appears to like his lunch." Matt continued his argument. "But what if he can only recollect bits and pieces of his past? Mrs. Sweeney chided him for making fun of our passion for the Cubs when he doesn't miss a single game. And he even said we couldn't interview him when a game was on. That's a whole lot of Cubs history stored in his head. Maybe there's no room left for anything else."

"That would be sad for him."

"For us, you mean."

"Huh?"

"Well, what kind of grade do you think an English teacher's gonna give us on our project if the only thing we turn in is a bunch of crap about a baseball team that hasn't won a championship in a million years?"

Jason slumped. "Whoa, I never thought of that. We're doomed."

"We're doomed all right," agreed Matt. "Unless we can get Abner to talk about his own life."

Their conversation was momentarily interrupted by the crack of the bat as "Boom-Boom" Banks drilled a batting-practice pitch out onto Waveland Avenue. From the boys' viewpoint, the street crowd below looked like enraged ants as they jostled for the souvenir.

"How are we going to get him to do that?" asked Jason. "How are we going to get him to talk about anything but the Cubs?"

"We just have to be more specific." Matt scrunched up his brow and fell into deep reflection for a minute or two. "I know. He was eighteen toward the end of World War I. I betcha he had to serve. Maybe he was a war hero. Teachers love to read about that kind of stuff."

"Yeah," said a suddenly enthusiastic Jason. "Maybe he fell on a grenade and saved his whole platoon."

Matt rolled his eyes. "Does he look like he fell on a grenade?"

Suddenly, without warning, the scoreboard shook. The boys were rocked as if they were on the Pair-O-Chutes at long forgotten Riverview Park. The seismic reaction was caused by "Boom-Boom" blasting one that screamed above the bleachers and plowed into the scoreboard some five hundred feet from home plate. Oddly, the ball struck the exact spot where "St. Louis" had been placed in the hand-operated board to keep track of their afternoon game against the Brewers. When one of the men who made a living climbing ladders and inserting metal numbers into various slots on the board reached the location, he discovered that the carnage was complete. The "St. Louis" plaque had been split in half by the force of the blow. The Cardinals had been—at least symbolically—knocked out of the National League. The bleacher crowd cheered wildly.

Strange events such as this one were now occurring with eerie regularity. In fact, the prodigious blow by Banks resulting in the demise of "St. Louis" was not the most talked-about topic on sports radio that day. Just an hour before game time, it was announced that center fielder "Shorty" Wilson had been suspended for thirty days for violating MLB's strict no-alcohol-in-the-clubhouse policy. Apparently, the diminutive outfielder was caught sipping from a bottle of gin before a game during the past week, and a search resulted in a veritable bar being found in his locker. Commissioner Bush came down hard so as to make an example of him. In a noon press conference televised live on ESPN, Bush said, "Drinking of alcohol by players in the clubhouse before, during, or after games will not be tolerated." A banner behind Bush blared out: Mission Accomplished. Commentator A.J. Pierzynski simply smirked.

The ball club had been warned in enough time to call up a rookie from Iowa to replace Wilson, and the newcomer was immediately inserted into the starting line-up. The youngster—whose name was Young—went 0 for 4 at the plate. However—and here's the weird part—he made two incredible catches in the top of the ninth inning to preserve the Cubs' 3-1 victory over New York.

The crowd, including a deliriously happy Matt and Jason, poured out into the streets of Wrigleyville, all abuzz about the game-saving catches. It was generally agreed upon that the slower Wilson would never have run down the balls, and that surely fate—for once—had intervened in favor of the Cubs. Meanwhile, the Brewers beat the Cardinals 7-2.

****

Abner, alone in his room, turned off the TV and stared thoughtfully ahead. In a flashback, he clearly remembered a rookie named Don Young costing the '69 Cubs a game in New York by dropping two fly balls in the ninth inning. Suddenly, a ghostly image seemed to grow out of the darkened screen. It was the scowling face of Leo Durocher, the manager of those ill-fated Cubs. Abner shook off the shock of seeing the scary skipper and slowly stood up. Something, he knew, was going on. Something he hadn't seen in his long, long life. Something very un-Cubs.

CHAPTER 6

"Now, remember the plan," Matt reminded his friend Jason as they walked toward the home. "We ask him about World War I. He probably fought in some major battles. Maybe he earned a Purple Heart or something cool like that. We'll have Mr. or Mrs. English teacher in tears."

Jason had purposely not worn his Cubs shirt again, so as to keep Abner's mind on the topic at hand. And Matt had gone over his eighth-grade history notes to refresh his memory on some of the key battles and famous generals. Both felt confident the plan would work.

It was an overcast day with significant rain in the forecast. The Cubs were in Philadelphia, preparing for a weekend series with the Phillies. Then, it was three with the Mets in New York. Early morning talk-show radio was inundated with callers who wanted to discuss recent Cub fortunes in what was still very early in the late-starting season. How was it possible, they argued, that the Cubs could lose such a talented player as Wilson and still go out and beat the Mets on the strength of a rookie's ninth-inning catches? How could they be only a game and a half out of first place? Was this young team really that good?

The boys walked through the entrance doors. Since their last visit, the place had been decked out in red, white, and blue for the Fourth of July, still a weekend away. Abby met them in the lobby.

"Hello, boys. Nice to see you again. But I have to warn you. Abner's in a weird mood today. I would have thought he'd be happy after yesterday's big win, but he's been quiet, kind of thoughtful. He even asked me—and this is very odd—what year it was. When I told him, he seemed surprised. He said he was positive it was 1969. I don't know what it means, but I guess at his age he's allowed a memory lapse now and then."

"Yes, Mrs. Sweeney, I suppose you're right," said Matt as politely as he could.

"Oh, don't be so formal. Please, call me Abby."

She steered them down a bright hallway toward the common area off the massive dining room. Here, a variety of options were available: an ice cream parlor, a library with comfortable chairs and a picture window facing an open field of wildflowers, a game room with chess and checker boards, and a billiards room. The latter was where many of the men gathered daily to shoot a game of eight ball and swap stories about their athletic feats from their younger years. These narratives were most likely exaggerated, but no one really cared to hear a truthful tale, the embellished version being far more interesting for the listener.

Abner was holding court in this room. Pool cue in one hand, chalk in the other, he was the natural focal point of the assemblage. After all, he was twenty-some years older than the next oldest men in the room, those born in the 1920s. When they were still infants, he had been a married man, a working stiff. He spoke from experience, from a wealth of knowledge. And he spoke in an old-world way that captivated his audience. For, as the boys were beginning to realize, the art of storytelling was Abner's greatest gift.

Abby stopped Matt and Jason at the door. "Listen," she said.

Abner's gravelly voice rang out. "That's how my daddy met Walt Disney's daddy. They were both hired laborers during the construction of the Columbian Exposition on the South Side in 1892. My daddy used to say the city never seen a sight like that old fair again. They called it the White City. With George Ferris' little invention towering over the Midway. So, as I was saying, Walt was born just a year and a half after me, and we played together before the Disney's up and moved to Missouri. That's on account of our daddies being such close friends."

Silence greeted Abner. Most of the men were awestruck, but one spoke out against him. "Oh, that's a crock. You never played with no Walt Disney."

Abner smiled. It was his standard reaction to anyone who doubted his personal history. "It's still a free country. Believe what you want."

But inwardly, Abner vowed revenge. Time to put this pup in his place. "Eight ball in the corner pocket."

Click. Game over.

Abby grabbed the boys by their arms. "Before I forget, Abner's celebrating a birthday a week from Tuesday, July 7th. He'll be one hundred twenty. A milestone to be sure. I want you two to join us for the party."

"Uh, okay," said Matt, not at all sure why they were being invited.

"Who's going to be there?" asked Jason. He was picturing a few of the ancients standing—or more likely sitting—around Abner and singing an off-key rendition of "Happy Birthday" as the old man hovered over a cake covered in candles. Lots of candles.

"Everybody," stated a confident Abby. "And I do mean everybody. As I said, he's turning one hundred twenty. That doesn't happen every day. Not only will all our residents be on hand, but all the local pols and paparazzi too. My guess is he'll make the front page of the *Trib* and the *Sun-Times*."

Matt and Jason had never considered the magnitude of an event such as this. Suddenly, they felt important. What other fourteen-year-old whelps had ever been invited to such a gala?

"Sure, we'll be happy to come," piped up Matt.

"Good. I'll include you on our guest list."

"What guest list?" A dour Abner had appeared in the doorway. "If this is for my birthday, they can come if they like. But I won't be here."

"And why might that be?" asked an amused Abby.

"It just so happens I've got other plans."

"And what might those be?"

"See, boys. This is what I get all the time around here. Everybody's always giving me the third degree when it ain't none of their concern." Often when angry, Abner's grammar slipped a little.

35

Now, he stared at Abby in a manner that suggested he was trying to make up his mind about something. When he spoke, it was if Patrick Henry had been reborn.

"All right, Miss Nosey-Pants, I'll tell you what my plans are. Remember how you badgered me to take those computer classes awhile back? Well, believe it or not, I've gotten so's I know my way around the Internet. I saved up my meager allowance that the warden grants me every month and went online—as the young folks say—to StubHub, where I bought myself a ticket to the opening game of the big Cubs-Cardinals series a week from Tuesday."

Here Abner paused and smiled a decidedly wicked smile. "That day, as you know, is my birthday, and for once I'm gonna celebrate it the way I want. Which, by the way, is not sitting around here all day listening to a bunch of people with gas problems praise me just 'cause I've been fortunate enough to live a few years longer than they have."

Abby stood aghast, her mouth wide open but no words coming out.

"Don't worry. I'm a big boy. I can take care of myself."

Finally, trying to grapple with the nightmare-in-progress, Abby spoke. Her voice was firm. "Now, Abner, you know it's strictly forbidden for you to go out of this complex without supervision."

"Watch me." With that, Abner turned and strolled toward the library, swinging his cane as if it was a walking stick. Looking back over his shoulder, he said, "Join me if you'd like, lads."

Matt looked toward a shaken Abby for direction. "Should we . . .?"

"Yes, go ahead if you want. He's had his say, and he certainly doesn't hold a grudge against you for keeping him under lock and key. Meanwhile, I'll have a chat with our director to see how we can solve this little problem." As if to justify Abner's outburst, she added, "I told you he was in a weird mood today."

Abby headed off toward the director's office. The boys had a dilemma. To join Abner in the library and force him to talk about World War I in his current disposition or to head home and eventually risk failing their first-ever high school English assignment. In the end, the decision was an easy one.

"Uh, Mr. Abner, sir? We're here, sir." Matt's normally strong voice was weak.

"Well, I can see that. C'mon in and take a seat. These chairs are quite comfy."

Matt and Jason slid softly across the green-carpeted room and sank into the plush lounge chairs. Abner smiled, not unkindly, in their general direction. No one spoke. The room's only other occupant, a heavyset gentleman with a neatly trimmed white beard, snored loudly, head thrown back and arms splayed to the sides. A hardbound copy of *Moby Dick* sat open on his lap. The rhythmic ticking of a grandfather's clock mimicked the in-and-out breathing of the exhausted reader.

Matt looked at Jason. Jason looked at Matt. They crossed their legs, trying to appear casual. Both silently cursed their fate: to spend the summer chasing after their elusive quarry, most likely to have their hopes—and grades—tossed overboard in the end.

"I see you two went to the ballpark yesterday."

The boys froze. How did he know that?

"Yes, sir," answered Jason hesitantly. "But, if I may ask, how did you know that?"

"Elementary," Abner answered. "If you look in any mirror, you'll see how sunburned your faces are. Red as lobsters. Oh, it's true, you might have been swimming, but the lake's bacteria levels have forced most of the beaches to close down this week, orders of Hizzoner. So, those faces plus the black on the soles of your shoes from walking on filthy cement—not to mention the traces of lead on Matt's fingers from nervously twirling his scorecard pencil throughout the game—tells me where you were."

Abby had told the boys that Abner never missed a thing. But this was surreal.

"We were there all right," said Jason, regaining his composure. "Great ending."

"Yes," said Abner softly. "Very different from the way I remember it."

37

"Huh?"

"Oh, never mind. You wouldn't be able to grasp it. I'm quite sure I'm alone in this quest. But I'll get to the bottom of it before this summer's out."

"Yes, sir," said Jason, completely unsure of what Abner was talking about.

"Well, I'm glad you enjoyed the game. I remember my first trip to that ballpark. It was in 1914, the year it opened."

"Wow!" exclaimed Matt. "You saw the Cubs play in Wrigley Field the year it opened?"

"Not exactly. I visited Weeghman Park on the corner of Clark and Addison. It was named for the man who built it, Charles Weeghman, and his team played there. And his team, by the way, was *not* the Cubs."

Here we go again, thought the confused boys.

"Who were they?" Jason asked impatiently.

"Not so fast," chuckled Abner. "Why don't you take a guess? A little trivial pursuit? The Cubs still played at West Side Park, a place they'd called home for years. So, my question is: for what team was the park that you know as Wrigley Field built?"

Matt and Jason were stumped. Abner sat back, folded his wiry arms across his chest, and waited. The clock and the other man's snoring continued unabated.

"The White Sox?" ventured Matt, knowing somehow that this couldn't possibly be the correct answer.

Abner yawned. "Not even close. They played at old Comiskey Park, which opened in 1910. At the time, it was considered the grandest stadium in the country."

The boys fell back into deep thought. The room began to close in on its occupants. Outside, it had begun to rain, and traces of water danced in crisscross fashion down the large window frame.

"Of course," said Jason, suddenly elated at having figured out the riddle. "It had to be the Bears. Ha. Good trick question, Mr. Abner. And I guess you know they played at Wrigley Field for fifty years."

Abner smiled. "Excellent answer, my boy. But incorrect, I'm afraid."

Jason sagged.

"Oh, you're correct in your knowledge that the Bears played there for a good half-century. From 1921 through 1970. The American Professional Football Association was founded in 1920, and before George Halas moved his team to Chicago, they spent their first season in the league as the Decatur Staleys."

"What?" asked an incredulous Jason.

"They even stuck with Staleys as their nickname during their first year in Chicago. The second year, 1922, the APFA became the NFL, and Halas' team became the Bears. The name was chosen to complement the other team that played there by then—the Cubs."

The boys were utterly discouraged. It was raining much harder now, and the water splashed against the window with reckless intensity.

"You boys ready to throw in the towel? Or should I say abandon ship? I thought so. Well, as we've discovered, it wasn't the Cubs, Sox, or Bears. Our beloved Wrigley Field was built for . . ." Abner paused, ". . . the Whales."

Lightning split the sky. Thunder crashed loudly, causing the window to vibrate. The sleeping gentleman stopped snoring. He shifted his considerable weight in the chair, and the book tumbled off his lap onto the floor. Still half-asleep, he mumbled in a raspy voice, "Call me Ishmael."

CHAPTER 7

Matt and Jason stared at the large pieces of battered fish on the plates in front of them. Alongside the home's "Fish on Friday" special sat a heaping mound of French fries, an ample portion of coleslaw, and a roll with butter. Abner had invited the boys to eat lunch with him; he even paid for the meals out of his expense account.

Abner didn't talk much, disregarding the boys' questions while he ate. He exhibited his usual healthy appetite and was, before long, swiping the last bite of roll over the remnants of tartar sauce on his otherwise clean plate.

"I see you boys can't like vinegar on your fries, the way they do it in England. Too bad. It gives 'em a better flavor than ketchup. But to each his own." Abner pushed his chair back and stretched out his legs, his hands coming to rest on his now full stomach. "Okay, ask away. I believe you had some questions about the Whales."

"Yes, sir," said Jason. "Who were they?"

Abner smiled. "I suppose that's a good opener. They were Chicago's entry in the Federal League, a third professional baseball league that started up in 1914. They were called the Chi-Feds in that first year."

"Well, how come we've never heard of them?" asked Jason.

"Probably because the entire league folded after 1915. Most people don't remember something that lasted only two or three years, kinda like the Edsel."

"So," asked Matt, "were they any good?"

"Good enough to finish in second place the first year and win it all the next. That was 1915, where they finished exactly .001 percentage point ahead of the St. Louis Terriers to claim the pennant. One of their best pitchers that year was good old

'Three-Finger,' who had a 17-8 record. Not bad for an old guy."

"Brown played for the Whales?" asked Jason.

"So did Joe Tinker. He was their player-manager both seasons. You see, the new league stole quite a few players from the established leagues. Know how? They offered 'em more money, just like they do the free agents today."

"This is amazing!" Matt blurted out. "So, you were a fan?"

"I was. I'd probably be one today if the league was still around. Funny, it was one hundred five years ago that the mighty Whales were the toast of the town, and I remember it like it was yesterday. You'll see, boys. Someday when you get up in years, you'll have these vivid flashbacks—scenes from your youth—and all your senses will kick into high gear. Faces, voices, even smells. They all come alive again, and you'll swear everything happened last week. What did Yogi Berra say? 'It's déjà vu all over again.'"

The boys laughed.

Abner, however, turned suddenly quiet. He was, of course, thinking about the 2020 Chicago Cubs, déjà vu with a twist. Was it really happening?

"Mr. Abner," asked Matt, "how did the Cubs finally end up in Wrigley—er, Weeghman Park?"

"Well, when the Federal League finally gave up its ghost, Weeghman was allowed to purchase the struggling Cubs, and he just moved 'em in the next year. They played their first game there on April 20, 1916. Then, later in the decade, William Wrigley, Jr., the chewing gum magnate, bought the club. From 1920 until 1926, when it was finally named after him, it was simply called Cubs Park. Unoriginal, but still better than Big-Ass Corporation Field, like the names of parks today."

The boys laughed again, a hollow echo bouncing off the walls. They looked around the dining room. Save for the three of them, it was empty. Abner had done it again. He had a refreshing way of speaking which had kept them spellbound for well over an hour. Thus, it came to them the realization that he had duped them into listening to more of his silly old baseball stories to the exclusion of his more significant, worldly experiences.

Enough was enough. Matt cleared his throat. "What was World War I like, sir?"

"Oh, that was awful. A terrible thing, war. Such a monumental waste of human life."

At last, thought the boys. Their plan was going to work.

"In fact, I've got quite a fascinating story about my participation in the Great War, as folks called it then."

Matt reached down quickly and pulled his notebook from his backpack.

"I had turned eighteen," Abner began, "gone through a pre-induction physical, been classified 1-A, and then it came in the mail. My official draft notice."

"When was that?" asked Matt as he furiously scribbled the valuable information on his writing pad.

"November 11th, 1918."

Matt started to record the date. He hesitated, looking slowly up into the grinning face of Abner.

"November 11th, sir?"

"That's right. Armistice Day. I received my draft notice on the very day the 'war to end all wars' ended. Talk about pullin' a horseshoe out of your butt. Or was it divine intervention? Probably not. I mean, why should the good Lord spare me when so many were lost?"

Back to square one, thought an exasperated Matt. They just couldn't seem to get anything historical out of Abner.

"One other remarkable thing happened that fall besides the end of the fighting."

Maybe, thought Matt, pen once again poised over paper.

"For the first time, the baseball season was shortened due to the government's 'Work or Fight' order. They finished up in early September, and two legendary teams met in the World Series—the Cubs and the Red Sox."

"Really?" asked Matt, swallowing the bait.

"Scout's honor," pledged Abner, and he was off and running. "Most people today wonder what it would be like to have

Fenway and Wrigley co-host a World Series, but even if those folks were around in 1918, they wouldn't have seen it."

"What? Why not?" asked Jason.

"Because our North Side playpen was deemed too small. So, the Cubs rented Charles Comiskey's South Side palace in order to sell more tickets."

"You're kidding," said a suspicious Matt. "The Cubs hosted a World Series in the White Sox home park?"

"They did indeed. One thing has never changed about the 'Grand Old Game' throughout the years, boys, and that's the owners' desire to make more money than they already have.

"That's why," Abner continued, "when the Cubs were closing in on the pennant in 1984, and everyone was in such an uproar about Wrigley not having lights and maybe having to play the home games for the World Series at Comiskey Park, I just said to myself, 'Been there, done that.'"

"You were there?" asked a skeptical Matt.

"I was. Game 1. Grandstand seats on the first-base side. That first game set the tone for the rest of the series. A 1-0 shutout for Boston. They would score only nine runs to the Cubs' ten but still win the six-game series, four games to two. Oh, and there were no home runs either."

The boys were having trouble digesting all these incredible facts. Apparently, they knew nothing about the history of the baseball team whose progress they followed daily.

"You boys know who the winning pitcher was for the BoSox in Game 1?"

They obviously didn't.

"Babe Ruth."

"*The* Babe Ruth? Babe Ruth the hitter?" asked Jason.

"No, this was Babe Ruth the pitcher. His pitching record is what sets him apart from all the greats who ever played the game. So, if some wiseacre tries to tell you that Ted Williams was the best player in history—or Mickey Mantle or Hank Aaron or Joe DiMaggio or Willie Mays—just ask them one question: exactly how many games did any of them win as a pitcher in the majors? The Babe won 94, for a .671 winning percentage. No telling how many he would have won if he'd stuck to pitching. Not bad for a fellow who also had a .342 lifetime batting average and 714 home runs."

Abner had made his point. Babe Ruth wasn't some mythical being, the Zeus of the American League. He was a multi-talented pitcher/hitter/outfielder who never struck out over a hundred times in a season and would probably wonder why so many players today were being paid millions of dollars to do just that.

Although the fish on their plates had long since gone cold, Matt and Jason sat spellbound. Had the man who sat across from them really seen Babe Ruth pitch a shutout against their beloved Cubs in a World Series game?

"Like I said," Abner began again, "the Bambino was quite a hurler. Beat the Cubs in Game 4 too. And when a pitcher named Carl Mays earned *his* second win in Game 6, the baseball season was over, just like that. It was only September 11th. Hard to believe they'll be playing well into November this year. Probably get snowed out and have to make it up next year. Hey, you boys haven't finished your fish and chips yet."

It was true. Their appetites had waned in the onslaught from Abner. The young scholars hadn't learned a thing about World War I. Ditto any special relationship Abner had had as a teen, perhaps with a gang of hooligans who wandered the streets and created mayhem by stealing fruit from the neighborhood vendors.

Matt looked at his friend. Jason looked as shell-shocked as if he had just survived some of those famous World War I skirmishes that Abner had miraculously avoided. This particular battle, it seemed, was a losing endeavor. They would never get anything out of Abner that they could use in their report.

"There's something I want to say to you boys."

There was more?

"I want to tell you that I was wrong to misbehave in such a reprehensible fashion earlier today. I think the world of Abs, and I shouldn't have mistreated her. She was justifiably upset when I told her I'm planning to blow off her little shindig to go to the game, and I fully intend to apologize to her later. That having been said, I'm still going. I can't miss some Cubs-Cardinals action just when the pot's comin' to a boil."

Balancing himself with his cane, Abner rose from the table. He looked and acted renewed, the opposite of how the weary teens felt. "I'm glad we had this little chat today. And now, if you'll excuse me, I'm off to play some shuffleboard. Do me a favor and put the trays away, will ya? Maggie throws a hissy fit when I leave 'em out."

CHAPTER 8

The opening game of the series between the first-place Cardinals and the second-place Cubs was the matinee of a day-night doubleheader, a rescheduled affair due to a rainout in May. In the glory days of Major League Baseball, *real* doubleheaders were treats for the fans, two-for-the-price-of-one extravaganzas that usually guaranteed at least one win for the home team. The '69 Cubs played fifteen such contests, and fourteen of those were scheduled at the start of the season. The Mets played twenty-two that same season. By the beginning of the twenty-first century, none of the thirty teams would give away any of their eighty-one home games. Why should they? If the owners could lure two different sets of fans to pay for each game separately—with a few hours in between to clean the park—then they would suck in twice the money. The message was clear: MLB loves its fans, but it loves them more when they pay up the nose for tickets, parking, food, drink, and merchandise.

The latter commodity exploded onto the market some forty years ago and increased exponentially in volume with each passing decade. Before long, every ballpark and mall in the nation had a store that sold team paraphernalia in sizes for men, women, and children. Three-month-old infants sat up proudly in their high chairs wearing FUTURE CUBS FAN bibs, were tucked in at night decked out in PHILLIES FOREVER jammies, or even did what babies do in their official YANKEES pinstriped diapers, giving new meaning to the term "Bronx Bombers." Actually, as Yankee management astutely assumed when they put the diapers on the market, they turned out to be a bigger selling item in the home cities of all the other teams and a special favorite of new moms and dads who happened to be

Red Sox fans. (True to franchise form, the Yankees didn't care if they were hated as long as they won.)

Adults, too, were crazy for all things baseball: caps, shirts, jerseys, even leather jackets. In recent years, motorcyclists had arrived at their annual bash in Sturgis, South Dakota, having forsaken traditional black and silver in favor of team colors and logos. Most conspicuously, California's infamous Hell's Angels showed up to the fest wearing red and white jackets emblazoned with LOS ANGELES ANGELS of ANAHEIM in ORANGE COUNTY, the team's newest name-of-the-month.

This and similar ploys were used by teams to keep rabid fans on the hunt for more stuff when their closets were already stuffed. Change your team's name from the Florida Marlins to the Miami Marlins. Or change your uniform colors from purple and teal to red and black as the Arizona Diamondbacks had done. Or switch from plain uniforms to pinstripes and back again. Or wear colored "softball" jerseys on Sundays and different colored caps on holidays. And make sure, each spring, that you trot out the biggest stars in the game to model the newest look like a crowded runway at a Victoria's Secret fashion show. And insist that the public pays more for the superstar's name and number on the back of the jerseys for sale even though it's most likely he'll skip town next season to sign with another team for more money.

Yet, somehow, all this greed could not spoil baseball. It was still, with all its imperfections, the perfect game. And Abner, not having been to the ballpark in some time, was looking forward to his birthday visit. Had he adhered to his original plan of walking out the front door—nothing surreptitious about an old gentleman going out for a walk, was there?—hailing a cab, and eventually taking his seat within the "Friendly Confines," he would have been more than a little disappointed. The relatively cheap ticket which he had purchased online was directly behind a pole, one of the distinct disadvantages for fans attending a game in a park that some claimed was as old and worn out as the Parthenon.

But Abby had come to the rescue. In the end, it hadn't been difficult at all to convince the Cubs' brass to make Abner their guest of honor on his one hundred twentieth birthday. He would, therefore, not be sitting behind a pole but rather in a skybox suite alongside the Ricketts family and other luminaries. Abby was sure that, when she told him, Abner would again make a fuss about all the hoopla, but that he would readily acquiesce when confronted with the comforts of the private box in contrast to a seat facing a slab of pockmarked concrete. King Theo was even sending his personal car to pick up Abner and Abby, who would be going along to watch over her patient. The kindly nurse dared to imagine that, although Abner had already celebrated one hundred nineteen birthdays, this one might be the best one yet.

****

It had been a week since Matt and Jason had visited Abner. They had been distracted by Fourth of July festivities, which had begun two nights earlier with the opening of a carnival on the grounds of Evanston Township High School. Tonight, they would visit the fairgrounds again, on the prowl for nubile girls who might be willing to take a turn on the tilt-a-whirl or a romantic ride to the top of the Ferris wheel with them. Girls to whom they could show off their athletic prowess by hurling softballs at shelves of grinning cats, thereby winning teddy bears for them. Girls with whom they could spread out blankets on worn patches of grass and listen to retro bands relive past glories. Girls who would melt like April snow in their arms when they snuggled up to watch the fireworks color the night sky.

The boys were exclusively interested in "new" girls, girls who had attended other elementary schools in their district but would now be joining them in high school. The reason for this was not complex. Girls with whom they had grown up had ceased to be exciting and had become—well, boring. Only a fresh face could move them to pay attention, could cause them to be on constant alert for "the" girl who possessed the power to change their mundane lives in an instant. Thus, the nightly quest.

"Did you see those two over by the lemonade stand? They were incredibly hot. Maybe they'll be there again tonight." Jason fell back onto Matt's bed, tucking his hands under his head as he did so.

"Dream on, lover boy." Matt sat on the floor, his back against the closet door. The television in the corner beamed the Cubs game. "I tell you now what I told you last night. They're high school girls."

"We're high school guys."

"No, we're high school freshmen—barely. Those girls were at least juniors. Did you see what they *weren't* wearing? They'd have laughed in our faces if we'd approached them."

"Maybe."

Matt rolled his eyes. It had been a rough week for the pair. They had struck out two nights in a row at the carnival, and their baseball team had lost four of six on the road trip and was already down 6-1 in the fourth at home against the Braves. If all that heartache wasn't enough, they didn't have a clue how they were ever going to get Abner to open up to them about his life.

Just as the boys watched in dismay as the Braves scored yet another run, Matt's cell phone rang.

"Hello?"

"Hi, Matt, this is Abby Sweeney over at the home. I need to tell you something."

Matt's first thought was an obvious one. Something had happened to Abner. Something bad. It could have been anything. A heart-attack. A stroke. A fatal fall. How terrible that such a thing would occur just days before his birthday. The tears that sprang suddenly from his eyes were a not-so-subtle sign of the boy's feelings for the old man. Jason watched in horror from the bed.

"What happened to Abner?" asked Matt, barely choking out the words.

"Oh, Matt, please forgive me. I didn't intend to startle you. Nothing's wrong with Abner. He's fine. Perfectly fine."

49

Matt breathed a sigh of relief. Quickly wiping a tear from his cheek, he gave a thumbs-up to Jason. "Thank goodness."

"Yes," said Abby, "thank goodness for every day we have with that irascible old man." The tenderness in Abby's voice was obvious. "I actually called to give you some good news. If you and Jason are available, Abner would like you two to be his guests at the Cubs game this coming Tuesday afternoon. Free of charge. The Ricketts family has invited him to sit in a skybox with them."

"Oh, my. Well, sure. I mean, we'd love to go," said a nearly speechless Matt.

"Go where?" asked an anxious Jason.

"I'll tell you in a minute," answered Matt, briefly cupping his hand over the phone. "Abby, are you there? Please tell Abner we'd be thrilled to go. Honored, that is."

"Great. I'll give him your answer. Be here by ten o'clock sharp. I'll be going along as well. It should be quite a day."

****

And it was. The bright blue limo with the red and white Cubs logo on both sides pulled up to the home at exactly ten o'clock. Abner wore a bright pink polo, a navy-blue blazer, tan slacks, and sensible shoes. Matt and Jason both wore the familiar home jerseys with names on the back—Brown and Banks respectively—and Cubs caps.

"You boys figure on playing today?" teased Abner, who thought dressing up for the game was absurd. "I suppose as long as you don't paint your faces like a bunch of ninnies, you can tag along."

Face painting was relatively new to the world of sports. Throughout Abner's childhood, adulthood, and a good portion of his early senior years, men dressed in blazers, ties, and hats to attend a game. The very thought of a grown man showing up at a sporting event looking like Darth Maul was something utterly unfathomable to anyone with a sense of style and grace. And Abner had both.

Matt and Jason had never ridden in a limousine before. Mr. Ricketts had stocked the car with Cracker Jack and cans of Pepsi, and the boys didn't think twice about helping themselves to the refreshments. Arriving at the ballpark, they were met by an usher who escorted them to a waiting elevator.

Abner was having the time of his life. When Abby had told him about the new arrangements, he hadn't been upset in the least. In fact, he was quite pleased that she had gone to so much trouble just so he wouldn't have to ask the person sitting next to him during the game what was happening on the field.

The group followed the usher along the catwalk leading to their luxury suite. Boos from the old grandstand section below greeted them as they made their way. This was a Wrigley tradition as ingrained in the fans as throwing back opposition home run balls or singing "Take Me Out to the Ball Game" for the seventh-inning stretch while paying homage to an oversized caricature of the late Harry Caray. The people in these seats were perpetually angry about having a good portion of their view blocked by the overhanging suites—as if the poles weren't bad enough. And although Abner would have normally sided with the common folk, he was feeling mighty special today, privileged one might say. So, as a gesture of good will, he leaned over the railing, raised his cane, and blessed them as if he was the pope and they were the multitudes gathered in St. Peter's Square. The booing increased. Someone yelled, "Get lost, old man!"

Abner turned to the others and feigned indignity. "Ingrates. And to think I almost fought in the Great War for their kind."

The Cubs and Cardinals had been waging a great war of their own for well over a century. All across the plains of Illinois, in towns such as Peoria, Springfield, and Quincy, the struggle pitted brother against brother and father against son in a mighty conflict reminiscent of the American Civil War but without the body count. Whenever the Cards came to town, legions of their fans, bedecked in red and white, would swarm up Interstate 55 to invade Wrigley like a pestilence of old. They behaved, for the most part, like benign—if unwelcome—relatives, never

51

resorting to fisticuffs in the stands when a polite, "How many times has your team won the World Series?" would quickly quiet the most ardent Cubs fan. And, in fairness to the red devils, they had always been true and faithful fans, knowledgeable about all the intricacies of the game.

So, the tension in the ballpark was palpable on Abner's one hundred twentieth birthday. In spite of a bad road trip and a 12-2 loss to the Braves to open the home stand, the Cubs had won both weekend games and were now poised to catch the Cardinals, sitting four games out with a four-game series soon to be underway.

The genial usher held open the door to the suite. Inside the lavishly decorated room were a giant screen television and a fully functional bar. On one side, tables had been set up to hold an array of hors d'oeuvres, including fresh shrimp cocktail. Sometime during the third inning, these would be replaced with hot entrees: Italian beef sandwiches, fish filets, lasagna, and Chicago-style hot dogs complete with poppy seed buns.

Mr. Ricketts stepped forward, clasped Abner's hand in his and said, "Mr. Tripplehorn, allow me to welcome you and your guests to Wrigley Field."

Introductions were made all around. Celebrities in the booth included the usual suspects: Bill Murray, Jim Belushi, and Mike Ditka, who was there to—unfortunately—sing during the stretch.

"Please, step outside so you can see the view." Mr. Ricketts opened the glass door, and the foursome stepped outside to where a few rows of seats looked out onto the sun-drenched field.

"Magnificent," said Abner in a barely audible voice. His eyes scanned the regal beauty of the pristine ballpark. The Cardinals were taking batting practice, and their red caps and sleeves complemented the green of the grass and the ivy-covered walls, a kind of Christmas in July. The old man looked out toward the scoreboard in center field, which rose majestically out of the multi-colored apparel of the bleacher crowd. Looking toward right field, he focused on the electronic message board. There, in big block letters, were the words: WELCOME ABNER TRIPPLEHORN AND FRIEND. Probably due to the length of Abner's surname, the "s" at the end of friends had been cut off. Matt and Jason would spend most of the day debating who was Abner's "friend."

The rest of the game was spent alternately diving into the delicacies—including a huge cake for Abner with exactly one hundred twenty candles on top—and cheering the Cubs to victory over the hated Cardinals by the lopsided score of 8-1. "Rusty" Wood went the distance for his ninth win of the season.

On the way home in the limo, Abner fell asleep clutching his scorecard. Abby cautioned the boys not to wake him. He had just experienced the grandest birthday of his life; he needed some rest.

CHAPTER 9

A bner slept through the nightcap, which the Cubs won 5-3 to sweep the pretend doubleheader. He also slept through breakfast; no one at the home ever remembered him doing that. His dreams—not surprisingly—were little-boy dreams of playing ball with his childhood heroes. The announcer's voice faded in and out like an old-time radio. "The Cubs lead the Pirates 2-1 with one man gone in the top of the ninth, but the Bucs have the potential tying and go-ahead runs on first and second. And look who's coming to the plate. It's the Flying Dutchman—Honus Wagner. He's 0 for 3 today, so look out. He's due. Tripplehorn looks in for the sign. He's been almost untouchable today. Here's the pitch. Whoa! A fastball that knocks Wagner down! I guess Tripplehorn doesn't want the fearsome slugger crowding the plate on him!"

Abner rolled over in bed and smiled. In life, he may have had to rely on a cane to get around, but in his dreams . . . "Wagner stares out toward the mound. He looks none too happy, pappy. Now he's back in the box. If he grips that bat any tighter, we'll have a pile of sawdust on home plate. Ha. Ha." (Announcers always chuckled at their own bad jokes; it was a baseball tradition.) "Here's the next delivery. It's a curveball. Hard-hit grounder to short. Tinker gloves it—to Evers—to Chance. This one's in the books, folks. What a finish!"

Abner Doubleday Tripplehorn stood on the mound surrounded by delirious teammates. *His* teammates. They lifted him to their shoulders and carried him toward the clubhouse down the left-field line. Out ahead of the jubilant procession was a player wearing number 10 on his back, clicking his heels in rapturous joy. Abner looked into the cheering crowd, searching for someone he knew, but the faces looked unfamiliar. Had none of his loved ones come out to see him play? He looked out toward the left-field wall. To his surprise, it was no longer there; in its place was a cornfield. Old number 10 turned to look at Abner, doffed his cap, clicked his heels one last time, and disappeared into the swaying stalks. Startled, Abner lost his balance atop the parade of players. As he began to fall, he saw an angry Pirate fan hurl a baseball at his head. He tried to duck, but by now he was tumbling toward the ground in a free-fall. A shot of pain coursed through him as the ball struck him directly in the forehead. He felt warm blood run down into his eyes; he heard a woman scream; then all went black.

****

The room was white. Of this, Abner was sure. He was also certain of three other things: his head hurt; he was hungry; and he wasn't in Kansas anymore. Where, exactly, was he?

"You're in the hospital. You took a little fall." The voice was Abby's. Abner turned his head slightly to look into his favorite nurse's eyes. They were red from crying, but she seemed composed now.

Some of it started coming back. There had been the game, which he had won . . . the celebration . . . the cornfield? He tried to speak, but only a raspy gurgle came out.

"Don't talk. You need to rest," said a concerned Abby. "You've got some stitches in your forehead, but the doctor says you'll be fine in no time. I'm allowed to stay here with you until they let you come home."

How fine *was* Abner? This was Abby's fear. He had rolled out of bed and taken a nasty knock, gouging his forehead on the end table as he plunged to the floor. They had stitched him up and then scanned his brain for more serious injuries. None showed up. But that didn't stop Abby from worrying. Luckily, she had just been entering his room to wake him when the accident occurred. It was her Hitchcockian scream that had penetrated his dream. The paramedics had come quickly, and Abby had been immediately released from her duties to accompany him. She had not left his side since.

Abner closed his eyes and contemplated what had happened to him. It was a shame, he concluded, that the fall occurred the day after his special birthday. But that was life. Its never-ending ups and downs gave it a richness it would otherwise have lacked. Still, Abner's vanity had been pricked. Would he continue to attract attention from women at the home with a jagged scar zigzagging merrily across his forehead? Perhaps, he thought, he could get an eye patch and pretend to be a pirate. Ladies loved pirates.

The doctors at Evanston Hospital concurred that Abner should remain a few days for observation, and Abby was encouraged to resume her position at the home. But she decided that, although she planned to go home at night, she would take a leave of absence and keep Abner company during the day. After all, who else would visit him?

As it turned out, plenty of people. As predicted, both Chicago dailies had run a story about him, and seemingly everyone who was anyone wanted to meet Abner. A follow-up story about his mishap alerted the public as to his whereabouts. Consequently, during the next couple of days, well-wishers dropped by at an alarming rate, annoying Abner to no end. (At least that's what he said.) The Rahmfather shook his hand; Cardinal Corleone blessed him; best of all, King Theo brought him an autographed baseball with signatures from all the Cubs. Ringo Starr, in town to play Ravinia with his All-Star Band, shared a birthday with Abner—number eighty for the legendary drummer—and presented him with a worn pair of drumsticks from his days with the Beatles. President Hillary Clinton, buried deep in her re-election campaign, took time out from her overloaded schedule to send a "Get Well" card to the old man and bluntly requested his vote in November. Unbeknownst to her, Abner had voted Republican since he'd cast his first ballot for Calvin Coolidge in 1924. But he appreciated the card nonetheless.

The flowers were nice too. The most lavish arrangement was sent from his friends at Serenity Now Retirement Community. The attached card wished him a speedy recovery and admonished him to "Leave the Nurses Alone." Also, the cafeteria staff sent him plates full of goodies when they heard that he'd complained—loudly—about the "awful" hospital food.

On Sunday morning, the doctors declared Abner healed and gave their permission for him to check out on Monday. The stitches had been removed, and there were no signs of a concussion. Abby felt comfortable leaving him, so—finally— he could relax and watch the Cubs-Brewers game in solitude. The Cubs had ended up losing the last two games of their series with St. Louis and had split their first two with Milwaukee, leaving them at five and four on the ten-game home stand. So, today's game was really, really big.

Abner sat up in his bed, braced by two pillows—*his* pillows, brought over by Abby—with a plate of cookies on his lap. He was focused on the big-screen television as the incomparable Wayne Messmer belted out the final words of the National Anthem. This was sweet, he thought. Private room. No interruptions.

Just then the door opened slowly. What now? thought Abner. Suddenly, his face brightened. "Well, if it isn't Spanky and Alfalfa. Where have you boys been?"

Matthew Holmes and Jason Doyle timidly approached Abner's bedside. Matt carried a homemade peach pie in his hands, compliments of his mother.

"We're sorry we didn't come sooner," said Jason. "Our moms wouldn't let us. They said you shouldn't be bothered."

"That's okay. Most days it was too crowded in here anyways. Good to see you."

"My mom baked you this," said Matt, holding out the pie.

"It looks good. Set it over there with the rest." Abner gestured to a table in the corner. It was packed with an assortment of cookies, candies, and the like. "Tell your mom I said thanks."

"Hey, where'd you get the cool drumsticks?" asked Jason.

Abner grinned. "Oh, just a present from a birthday buddy. Pull up a chair."

The boys plopped down into cushy chairs by the window. The aroma of fresh flowers assailed them.

"Nice flowers," said Matt, trying to be polite.

"Yes, they give the room a sense of beauty that it pines for. Covers up the stale bedpan smell too. You want some cookies?"

For the next few hours, the friends sat uninterrupted, at least by hospital standards. A jovial nurse burst in once each hour to check Abner's vitals, but otherwise it was uncommonly quiet. Matt and Jason paid close attention to the game, not allowing Abner's occasional snoring to bother them. Once, when he started from a deep sleep during a commercial break, the boys told him he had missed an eight-run uprising by the Brewers. When the last ad ended, Abner was surprised to see the Cubs still leading 3-0. Stifled giggles in the room alerted him to the prank, and he laughed so hard he had a coughing fit.

The situation wasn't so funny, however, when the defense imploded in the top of the eighth, allowing Milwaukee to put four unearned runs on the board and take the lead, a lead that would cost "Jolly" Jenkins his tenth win. In true Cub-like fashion, their last six batters failed to reach base, a sorrowful ending to a sunny day.

When the final out was recorded, a weak tap back to the pitcher by Banks, there was no controlling Abner's wrath. It was a good thing the nurse didn't barge in to take his blood pressure during the tirade.

"Why, those bums! Those good-for-nothin' bums! You see, boys, what crappy defense will do for you? When teams are built, everybody wants sluggers, big lunks who can drive the ball out of the park. But what good does that do if those same jackhammers drop pop-ups and muff ground balls?"

Abner stopped to rest his jaws. He was breathing heavily, frighteningly so for a man his age who was already lying in a hospital bed hooked up to monitors. Both boys found themselves staring at the giant red EMERGENCY button hanging loosely from the back of the bed.

Breaking the tension, Abner chuckled. "Sorry, boys. Didn't mean to get so worked up. It's not like they haven't blown one before. They'll bounce back. Plenty of time." Abner feared that, although there might be time left for the Cubs, there might not be much time left for him.

"That *was* incredibly bad defense though," said Matt, tacitly agreeing with every word of Abner's outburst.

"Ah, that was nothing. Not as bad as '29. Hoo-wee, that was one for the record books."

"What happened in '29?" asked a curious Jason.

Abner reached for the water cup on the tray beside his bed and sipped from the straw. He seemed relaxed now, confident, like a college professor who had his material down cold—and these kids had so much to learn.

"Defense, boys. Better make that *bad* defense. That's what cost the Cubs a World Series. They were playing the Philadelphia Athletics, a chance for revenge since the A's had beaten them four games to one in 1910, using only two pitchers in the five contests. Plus, it was the first time in eleven years since the Cubs had won an N.L. pennant. Imagine, an entire decade come and gone without a pennant on the North Side. Why, it was unheard of back then."

Matt and Jason exchanged envious glances.

"It was a great Cubs team too. The top three pitchers—Charlie Root, Guy Bush, and Pat Malone—averaged twenty wins among them. And the outfielders were even better. Riggs Stephenson, Hack Wilson, Kiki Cuyler—all hit in the mid-.300s, and each had over 100 RBIs."

"Excuse me," Matt asked, "but did you say Wilson and Cuyler?"

Only mildly irritated at having been interrupted, Abner stared at Matt in an odd way. "The clouds are beginning to part for you, are they? Well, let's not get ahead of ourselves. Time will tell. Time will surely tell."

Matt thought, . . . do do do do . . . do do do do . . . next stop, "The Twilight Zone."

"As I was saying, the pitching and hitting were there. Second baseman Rogers Hornsby hit .380 that year. You think any of the Bozos who earn twelve million a year could do that today?"

Abner was right. It had been awhile.

"They had a great manager as well—Joe McCarthy. He'd go on to win multiple championships with the Yankees. But all that good couldn't make up for poor play in the field, especially at crucial moments. They say every World Series turns on a single play, whether it happens in the first game—like Willie Mays' catch in Game 1 of the '54 series or Kirk Gibson's pinch-hit homer to close out the '88 opener—or in some other game along the way."

Abner paused; sadness seemed to touch his spirit. "For the Cubs in '29, it was Game 4. In Philly. The A's won the first two games at Wrigley; the Cubs took Game 3 in their park. So, the A's led the series two games to one. But with the Cubs leading 8-0 at stretch time, the series was as good as tied. C'mon, there was no way a team as great as this could ever blow an eight-run advantage so late in the game."

"They didn't?" asked a mortified Jason.

"Oh, but they did. Hack Wilson misplayed two fly balls that were sure outs, the second one for a three-run, inside-the-park homer. Maybe, as everyone surmised, he lost 'em in the sun. Maybe he just wasn't feeling right that day."

"What do you mean by that?" asked Matt.

"He was a drunk. Today, we'd probably refer to him as having a problem with alcohol. McCarthy said he never knew from which direction Hack would arrive at the ballpark each morning. All depended on which establishments he'd hung out at the night before. Mostly Capone's joints; he and Al were pals. In 1930, the year after his infamous errors, Hack hit 56 home runs and drove in 191. The homers held up as the N.L. record 'til the steroid era, and the 191 RBIs will most likely stand forever. But he was washed up at age thirty-four. And he died penniless at forty-eight. Still made the Hall of Fame though.

"Anyway, the A's scored ten in the bottom of the seventh and won the game 10-8. It would forever be referred to as the 'Mack Attack' in honor of Manager Connie Mack, who never wore anything but a three-piece suit and a straw hat when he managed. Not a bad idea for some of these big-bellied skippers today. Those uniforms just don't make 'em look good."

"I take it the Cubs just gave up after that," said a forlorn Matt.

"Not exactly. They weren't quitters. Just hapless. They took a 2-0 lead into the bottom of the ninth in Game 5, hoping to take the series back to Chicago. But it wasn't to be. The A's, who were an outstanding team, scored three to claim the series."

"Were you at any of the games?" asked Jason.

"Yes, Vera and I attended the first two at home. As I said earlier, both losses."

Had the boys been "listening between the lines," they would have leapt at the chance to learn more about the real Abner. He had just mentioned his wife's name to them for the first time, and all they were thinking about was an alcoholic outfielder, a ten-run explosion, and the ongoing saga of one of the National League's original teams.

And, that night, visions of baby bears danced in their heads.

CHAPTER 10

July turned out to be a scorcher, one of the hottest in recent memory. And although the 2020 Cubs didn't play day baseball every day as the '69 Cubs had done, they began to wilt in the heat just as quickly. "Rusty" Wood lost ten miles per hour off his fastball, and "Squats" Hartnett lost twelve pounds of body weight. "Hammering" Hack and "Boom-Boom" Banks watched blasts that had easily soared out of Wrigley a month ago now die languid deaths on the warning track. During one night game, when the temperature dropped below a hundred for the first time in a week, "Sober" Sutter wore his "lucky" long underwear out to the bullpen and fainted from heat exhaustion even before he was summoned to pitch. The fast-thinking trainer scooped Frosty Malts into him until his body temperature returned to normal.

Injuries, the wild card in every baseball season, took their toll as well. The outfield was decimated when "Stretch" Williams forgot to do just that and pulled a hamstring running down a ball in the alley. Two days later, "Chubby" Cuyler attacked a Gatorade cooler with a bat, spraining both wrists. With "Shorty" Wilson still suspended, stuck in daily AA meetings, the outfield was being patrolled by minor leaguers. The results were predictable. One rookie ran out from under his cap attempting a shoestring catch, somersaulted across the grass, and came up without the ball. By the time he located it, resting comfortably *inside* his cap, three Dodgers had scampered home.

But exhaustion and injuries had always been part of the game. Unlike any other sportsmen, the "boys of summer" played every day for six months—not counting playoffs—and were expected to overcome these trifles. At the professional level, it had never been a game for the weak of body or mind.

And just when a player felt he had conquered the game, just when his ego was being fed by his remarkable play, just when he felt he owned the game like no one before him, the ball jumped up and bit him, its venom coursing through his veins. But unlike an old warrior who received the fatal snakebite while hiding from his enemies in an isolated cave, the ballplayer's agony was always played out in public, never allowing him to die with dignity. Just ask Billy Buck.

Abner had witnessed slumps a million times—well, at least over a hundred. They aggravated his old bones. But it wasn't time to take a long walk off a short pier. Not yet. In July, it was impossible to tell—if one's team was doing poorly after starting out well—whether it was a temporary backslide or a permanent free-fall. But most fans of the 2020 Cubs were sure this was the end when the team fell back into third place behind the surging Cincinnati Reds. And, to make it worse, they were now seven games behind the Cardinals.

"Do you think it's over?" asked a disconsolate Jason.

"It ain't over 'til it's over," said Abner, quoting a well-worn Yogi-ism. But he wasn't so sure.

As he sat opposite Matt and Jason in the nursing home's ice cream parlor, he suspected this might be his last summer to find out if his Cubs were going to finally get over the hump of history. His recent fall had taken its inevitable toll, and, much like the weary ballplayers, his day-to-day grind now produced more pain and less pleasure. But, for now, he had to keep his young friends' hopes alive.

"The All-Star game's not 'til next week," said Abner, slowly slurping his strawberry soda. "Let's see where we stand then."

It was true, the boys conceded. With the season's late start due to the mysterious disappearance of the plane, there were still nearly three full months left after the break.

"Uh, Abner," said Matt, "what was the Great Depression like? How did you survive it?"

Again, the plan was for the boys to ask specific questions about historical events to force Abner to share his experiences, thus providing substance to their project.

"The Great Depression? Darn depressing," joked Abner, and the boys chuckled. "But who says I survived it? Who says anyone survived it? That decade was like a war in that, once you crawled through it, you never wanted to live like that again. It was ugly. Dirt ugly. I suppose the only thing that kept Chicago's spirit up was the 'three-year lock' the Cubs had going for themselves."

"The 'three-year lock'?" asked Matt. "What was that?"

"Why, that refers to the greatest long-term stretch of ball the Cubs played since the early part of the twentieth century. Every three years, just like a well-tuned Swiss watch, the North Siders 'locked up' the N.L. pennant. It actually began in '29, about a month before the Stock Market Crash. Then, they took it again in '32, '35, and '38, four times in ten seasons."

Matt set the spoon down into his hot fudge sundae. "The Cubs? Our Cubs?"

"Those would be the ones. And they were good all right." Here, Abner paused. "Just not good enough to win the World Series in any of those years. Of course, in '32, Babe Ruth had a lot to say about the outcome."

"Babe Ruth the pitcher?" asked Jason, confident he had it right this time.

"No, this was Babe Ruth the hitter. His last great hurrah. In fact, one moment from Game 3 sealed his status forever as the greatest sports legend who ever lived."

"The called shot!" exclaimed Matt.

"Well, I guess you young fellows aren't as ignorant of your nation's pastime as I thought you were."

"Heck," chimed in Jason, "everybody's heard about that! Did he really do it? Were you there?"

"Course I was there. What d'ya think, I was just a sit-at-home? My friend Gimper—we called him that 'cause he had a bum leg—well, anyways, he got us two tickets right down behind the first-base dugout. We was practically on the field."

Abner's grammar always faltered a bit when he got excited. The boys never noticed.

"October 1ˢᵗ, 1932. The ballpark was packed—about 50,000 fans saw that game."

"What?" yelled Jason. "How did they get that many into Wrigley Field?"

"I thought you might be a tad curious about that. Temporary bleachers were erected on Waveland and Sheffield Avenues. It was quite a sight!"

Matt and Jason tried to picture what that must have looked like. Or what it must have been like to see Babe Ruth and the mighty Yankees come to town.

"Well, the Babe and Lou Gehrig came out to take batting practice to a chorus of boos, and they responded to the jeers by hitting mammoth shots into the bleachers. Afterward, Babe supposedly said he would take half his salary if he could play all his games in 'this dump.' You see, there was a lot of bad blood between those two teams. Mark Koenig, a former Yankee infielder, had been picked up by the Cubs during the regular season, and even though he had helped them win the pennant, his new team voted for him to receive only a half-share of the World Series money. That extra dough was a big deal to players back then. Babe was furious. He said the Cubs were cheapskates."

"Were they?" asked Matt.

"Maybe. Looking back, all it did was piss off the Yankees. Probably not a good idea. So, anyways, that was the situation when Game 3 began with the Yanks already ahead two games to none.

"Babe came up in the first with two men on base. Well, the crowd went crazy. You'd thought it was Judas Iscariot at the bat. Babe just smiled and silenced the crowd with a three-run homer. Gehrig added a solo shot in the third. But the Cubs fought back. They scored the tying run in the fourth after Babe misplayed a ball in right. Man, the crowd was merciless then. But, you know, it didn't faze Ruth at all. He actually doffed his cap at the taunting crowd.

"The game moved to the top of the fifth; score tied 4-4. That's when it happened. One out and the bases empty. We could see the Cubs in their dugout from where we were sitting. Those players called Babe every name in the book and then some. Vulgar names you wouldn't think of calling your worst enemy. They even rolled lemons toward home plate to suggest the Sultan of Swat wasn't all he was cracked up to be."

"But he was, wasn't he?" asked Jason.

"That day, he was even more," Abner said, a knowing smile spreading across his face. "He didn't just take the pitches, you know. He kept a running count by signaling 'strike one,' 'strike two' with his fingers. After the second strike, with the count 2-2, he gestured or pointed or whatever it was. Some say it was toward the Cubs' dugout; others say it was at Charlie Root, whose name was soon to be forever linked with the legacy of the Babe. Even by studying the 8mm film footage taken by a fan that day, it's hard to tell. But unlike the Zapruder film of the Kennedy assassination, it doesn't really matter what the film suggests. It only matters what the legend says."

"He pointed to the center-field bleachers!" yelled Jason.

"And then hit one past the flagpole on the next pitch, 500 feet from home plate."

"And you saw it!"

"I saw it."

"Well," asked Matt, "did he point?"

"All I know for sure is that, right before he hit it, my friend Gimper turned to me and said, 'Did you see that? He just pointed to the bleachers. He's gonna hit one there.'"

"And what did you say?"

"I said, 'Wouldn't put it past him.' Funny thing, nobody remembers Gehrig hit one right after Ruth, his second of the day as well. The place was in shock. Wherever he went, the Big Fellow cast a big shadow."

Once again, Matt and Jason were knocked to the canvas. Eighty-eight years earlier, the man sitting across the table from them drinking an ice cream soda had sat in Wrigley Field on a sunny October day and witnessed the most famous event in World Series history. But that was just the tip of the iceberg.

It was slowly dawning on the boys that Abner was a living time capsule. Listening to him weave his splendid stories was somewhat like history. But not the kind of history that was taught in school. Not the kind made up of documents, expeditions, elections, and wars—unless it was a war of bean balls. The old man was teaching the boys a life lesson—that baseball had been intricately woven into the fabric of American life, never far away from the hearts and minds of the common person, who supported his team with a passion normally reserved for the sacred subjects of religion and politics. And if the Italians cheered with added vigor for Joe DiMaggio, as the Jews applauded the exploits of Hank Greenberg and the Negroes rooted for Jackie Robinson to succeed, it was because heroics in Major League Baseball paved the path of acceptance for each successive immigrant group into the vast melting pot of American society.

Abner interrupted their thoughts. "Did you know the called shot was Babe Ruth's last World Series home run?"

Another nugget to pocket.

"After two more seasons with the Yanks, declining in overall health from all of his, shall we say, appetites, Ruth finished his career with the lowly Boston Braves in the National League. His power had eroded considerably by then. But one day very near the end he left 'em with a final feat, probably just to remind the country that he was the one who had saved baseball from the fallout of the Black Sox Scandal of 1919."

"When the White Sox threw the World Series to the Reds," interjected Matt.

Abner looked astonished. "My, my. Give that kid a cigar."

Matt blushed.

"As I was saying, the Great Bambino rediscovered his stroke on a May afternoon at old Forbes Field in Pittsburgh. Hit three out. One cleared the upper-deck roof in right. A Ruthian blast if ever there was one. Added a single that day too. A few days later, he grounded out to first in Philly and called it quits." Abner, having led Matt and Jason down a rabbit hole of surprises once more, grinned a Cheshire grin. "So, boys, did you enjoy your ice cream?"

CHAPTER 11

The All-Star Game came and went. It was held in Oklahoma City, home of the Rays. They had, of course, originally played in Tampa Bay, but the crappy stadium—worst in MLB history—in conjunction with even crappier attendance—even during playoff seasons—had forced the Rays to move. The fact that they'd held onto their name and stingray logo in the middle of Oklahoma—"where the wind comes sweepin' down the plain"—made absolutely no sense whatsoever. But it hadn't been the first time in sports history that the "name game" had tripped up a team.

NBA fans had witnessed the pilgrimage of the Lakers from Minnesota—Land of 10,000 Lakes—to Los Angeles; and the Jazz had moved from New Orleans to, of all places, Utah, where they somehow forgot to change their nickname to the more appropriate Tabernacle Choir Boys. Major League Baseball, too, had seen those trolley-dodging Brooklyn Dodgers move to L.A., where nary a streetcar could be found, although dodging bullets from road-rage-afflicted drivers on the freeway probably resonated with some Californians. It was generally agreed upon by most Chicagoans, however, that if baseball ever went international and the Cubs moved to the Philippines, they'd have to change their name to the Manila Folders.

Several "new" Cubs had played in the annual classic, a 4-2 National League win. But none had been voted "starters" as most fans around the nation had not yet caught on that somehow, someway, this was meant to be a team of destiny. "Sober" Sutter did register the save, however, striking out the side in the ninth; and "Boom-Boom" Banks crushed a solo shot in the fifth that cleared the left-field upper-deck roof, reminiscent of the Babe's blast in Pittsburgh eighty-five years earlier.

But the most significant result of having so many Cubs sit out the game was that the injured players were rested and healthy to begin the second half of the season. The "opener" in Cincy would be the first time since "Shorty" Wilson's suspension that the entire roster of starters would take the field together. Commissioner Bush had cleared the happy-go-lucky, loved-to-get-drunky night owl to play, provided he continued to attend AA meetings whenever the Cubs were in town. On the road, he was to room with Sutter, who would attempt to convince Wilson to "Do the Dew."

"Do you think they can do it?" asked Jason. "Come back, I mean."

It was the end of July, the day after the All-Star Game, and the heat had broken. Matt, Jason, and Abner sat in the garden where they had first met.

"Come, come," said Abner. "Not to worry. Two behind the Reds and eight behind the Cardinals is nothin'. Why, in '35, the Cubs won twenty-one games in a row in September to steal the pennant from St. Louis. Now, *that* was a comeback."

"Twenty-one in a row?" Matt's mouth hung open, a chewed piece of gum balanced precariously near the tip of his tongue.

"Close your mouth, son," scolded Abner. "Yes, those were the days when a young broadcaster on WHO radio in Des Moines recreated—or rather, invented—the excitement of each play by first reading and then giving life to the telegraph messages as they came over the wire. Like this. 'There's a long drive, way back—and it's caught! A leaping grab just shy of the warning track!' Meanwhile, the folks at the ballpark were watching a lazy pop-fly to medium-deep center field."

"Wow, that took some imagination," said Jason, surprised that someone could actually make a game come alive in such a fashion.

"You bet your blue jeans it did. And this young broadcaster had it in spades. By the way, he eventually grew up to become our fortieth president."

"Huh?" said the boys in unison.

"Ronald Reagan was his name," Abner continued, "but he went by the nickname of 'Dutch.' People in those days felt confident they could, given time and hard work, be what they wanted to be. And, in spite of the Depression, the average Joe never gave up. Sooner or later, dreams often do come true. But you have to keep your eye on the prize. Instant gratification has never gotten anyone anywhere. You have to let life play out the way it's supposed to, one glorious day at a time."

Try as they might, it was difficult for the boys to grasp what Abner was trying to tell them. At their young age, it was impossible to see the big picture, to imagine what the future had in store.

"What I'm trying to say, boys, is work hard, do your best, and your dreams, whatever they might be, will hopefully come true. And as far as our beloved Cubs are concerned, if they come roaring back from behind and surprise everyone like it was 1935 all over again, we'll enjoy it. If they don't, c'est la vie."

Matt had a sudden brain-flash. "Mr. Abner, sir, did your dreams ever come true?"

Abner leaned back in the bench. He crossed one leg over the other and gazed up at the cloudless sky. When he spoke, it was in a soft, wistful voice. "Most of 'em, Matt. Most of 'em."

The following seconds were silent. The boys stared at Abner while Abner stared at the sunlit sky. His eyes began to water, and a single tear pushed its way out onto his cheek.

"Doggone sun," he muttered as he fumbled in his shirt pocket in search of sunglasses. He slipped them on, casually brushing away the lonesome tear as he did so.

Awkward didn't begin to cover it. Had Abby not burst onto the scene, it's doubtful the boys would have ever spoken another word.

"Would you men like some lemonade?" Abby produced a tray holding a sweat-soaked pitcher and three glasses. She poured for the group. "I suppose you're all talking baseball again. Abner's probably got you all caught up on the famous 'three-year lock,' huh?"

"You know about that?" asked a startled Jason.

70

"Well, you don't think Mr. Raconteur just jabbers away when you're here, do you? Trust me, I've heard all the tall tales—twice and then some."

Both boys laughed, and lemonade shot from Jason's nose.

Abner, back to his obdurate old self, sneered in Abby's direction. "Well, Miss Snoopy-Shorts, if you wouldn't spend half your working hours eavesdropping on your patients' private conversations, you would be able to complete your duties in a more efficient manner. So, if you're through disturbing the peace, why don't you go harass someone else and leave me and my friends alone to enjoy the day?"

"Oh," said Abby, who always gave it right back, "and which dwarf are we today? Let's see. Sleepy? No, you seem wide-awake. Sneezy? Are your allergies acting up again? He's allergic to pleasantries, boys. Bashful? Hardly. Oh, wait, I know . . ."

"Hardee-har-har," said Abner as Ralph Kramden.

"All right, I get the picture. I'll leave you three alone so you can solve the world's problems. Call me when there's peace in the Middle East, and I'll come pick up the tray."

The trio of friends—neither Jason nor Matt had missed it when Abner had used the word to describe them—sipped their lemonade, buoyed by the cool, late-afternoon breeze. Sometimes, things are best left unsaid—as the dust of distant memories is sometimes best left undisturbed.

Finally, Jason broke the silence. "Excuse me, sir, but what happened to the Cubs after they won the twenty-one games and clinched the pennant?"

"Well, in spite of the late-season surge, they still lost the 1935 World Series to the Tigers, four games to two. I guess it was Detroit's revenge for '07 and '08."

"But that was almost thirty years later," said Matt. "Who was still around for revenge?"

Abner chuckled. "Good point. None of the players, that's for sure. But some young Tiger fans who were now middle-aged probably thought it was great fun to watch the Cubs falter at the altar, so to speak."

"How *did* the Cubs mess up?" asked a perplexed Jason.

"Well, they weren't supposed to. They had everything: power, pitching, speed, defense; it was probably their best team since '08. And the momentum of the September streak. Plus, the Tigers had never won the World Series in four tries, including a seven-game loss to the Cardinals the year before.

"The 1st game at Navin Field in Detroit was all Cubs, a 3-0 shutout for twenty-game winner Lon Warneke. Then, in Game 2, which the Tigers won, their fearsome slugger Hank Greenberg broke his wrist on a collision at home with Cubs catcher Gabby Hartnett."

"Hartnett?" asked Jason.

Abner flashed a we've-been-through-this-before-so-there's-no-need-to-discuss-it frown in Jason's direction. "With their best hitter sidelined and the next three games slated for Chicago, it seemed like Detroit was doomed."

"But the Cubs still managed to lose," said Matt. A statement, not a question.

"The Tigers won the next two, Lon Warneke earned his second victory in Game 5, and it was back to Detroit. Game 6 was a 3-3 tie going into the ninth. Stan Hack, the Cubs great third baseman, led off with a triple." Abner paused. "And, yes, I said Hack. But he might as well have been stranded on an isolated island in the middle of the Pacific. Three up, three down. A two-out single in the bottom of the ninth won it all for the Tigers."

"It must have been Crazyville in Detroit," said Matt.

"It was. Understand this was mid-Depression, and Motown had been hit hard. Cars were still considered a luxury item. I think it was important for the city to celebrate something. Anything. And the party was just beginning. The Lions won the NFL Championship that winter, and the Red Wings brought home the Stanley Cup in the spring."

"Wow!" exclaimed Jason. "It would be cool for that to happen in Chicago."

"Perhaps someday. If you live to be my age," joked Abner.

Both boys pondered that for a moment. It would mean they would have to live for another one hundred six years. In the year 2126, would baseball still be the one "constant"—as James Earl Jones' character so eloquently proposed in the movie *Field of Dreams*?

"Let's take a stroll," suggested Abner, slowly rising to his feet. "These old bones get tired when they sit for too long. As long as you're with me, the guards will allow us to leave the yard to walk around the block."

Matt and Jason got a kick out of Abner's prison metaphors.

"But if I try to escape by crossing the street, they'll shoot first and ask questions later."

They stopped briefly at the lobby's restroom so Abner could relieve himself. "That darn lemonade always goes right through me." And then they were off.

The tree-lined street provided instant shade as the trio headed out, Gandalf with his staff leading Bilbo and Frodo on another perilous journey into the unknown. In some ways, Abner had already taken the boys on several amazing adventures through the past. And although he hadn't yet shared much—any?—of his *personal* past with them, Matt and Jason felt they had experienced more this summer than if they'd stuck to stalking girls and hanging out at Homer's. In fact, their very adolescent existence seemed a trifle boring compared to the energetic flow of Abner's everyday life. No matter what was happening, he always seemed up for it—or down with it, depending on what generation he was interacting with. It was as if he had discovered along the pathway of life that every minute was too precious to be wasted on the mundane.

"Hey, slow pokes, am I out for a walk by myself?"

Matt and Jason suddenly realized that Abner had widened the gap between them. Several giant strides caught them up.

"Step on a crack, eh?" chuckled Abner. "Look, if you youngsters are too tired to keep up with an old coot, then why don't you scurry on home and take a nap before dinner?"

Jason laughed. "Don't you ever take naps, Abner?"

Abner snorted. "Hmmph. Those little snatches of death? No, thank you. I get a good six hours a night. No need to overdo it."

The boys flashed guilty looks at one another. As healthy, active teens on summer vacation, they were seldom up after midnight, never up much before ten. And they occasionally took naps in front of the television.

"Besides," Abner added, "I'll have plenty of rest in the near future. The Lord's not going to let me stay down here forever. And one good thing for me, I probably won't die after a long, drawn-out illness. At my age, whatever knocks me down will most likely knock me out. Like a punch from Ali in his prime."

This was a stunning revelation. The boys had never considered Abner being there one minute, gone the next.

"Now, you take those poor people with Alzheimer's or Lou Gehrig's disease, they really suffer before they pass. And of all the folks who ever had Gehrig's, Lou himself probably suffered the most."

"Why?" asked Jason.

"Because he had the furthest to fall. Did you boys know he already had ALS but didn't know it when he played against the Cubs in the 1938 World Series?"

"The last year of the 'three-year lock' for the Cubs, right?"

"Right. And they captured the N.L. pennant in dramatic fashion, in some ways even more exciting than their September streak back in '35."

"How?" asked Matt, clearly fascinated with the fact that these Cubs of long ago seemed to be able to pull rabbits out of their hats whenever a magic moment was called for.

"You ever hear tell of the Homer in the Gloamin'?"

Once again, there were staggering holes in the boys' baseball knowledge.

Abner shook his head in mock dismay. "And some fools say education's in decline in this country—wonder where they got that notion? Well, grab onto your briefs, boys. Here we go again. September 28, 1938. Wrigley Field. The Cubs had been chasing down the Pirates all summer. The day before, they'd beat the Bucs 2-1 to pull within a half game of first. Going into the bottom of the ninth, it was all knotted up at 5-5. The men in blue convened to discuss the lack of light and decided that, if the Cubs didn't score, the game was over. Called on account of darkness. It would have to be replayed in its entirety as part of a doubleheader the next day."

The suspense of the retelling caused Abner to slow down and finally stop beneath an ancient maple. He turned to face the boys, and the sunlight-shadow mix that flickered across his weathered cheeks made him somehow look younger.

"Two men out. Nobody on base. An 0-2 count on player-manager Gabby Hartnett. One strike away from the Pirates going to bed still in first place. One thing you should know: the year before, they had added the brick walls and bleachers as fans basically know them today. A slightly shorter drive to the left-center field power alley."

"And that's what happened?" shouted a disbelieving Jason. "That's where he hit it?"

Abner scowled. "Well, I *did* say it was the Homer in the Gloamin', not the Double in the Dusk, didn't I?"

"Sorry."

"It's one of the most famous home runs in baseball history. The Cubs won 10-1 the next day for the series sweep, and they never looked back. Clinched the pennant a few days later."

"But the Yankees took the World Series again?" asked Matt.

"It's funny you should say 'again,' because it was their third-straight MLB Championship, the first team to ever accomplish that particular feat. They would win a fourth-one the next year. It kinda became a habit for them after awhile. By then, Joltin' Joe DiMaggio was their main man—as you youngsters like to say—and he would lead them through the forties until Mickey Mantle came along to fill his shoes. It was always revolve-a-star with the Yanks."

"And Gehrig?" asked a suddenly forlorn Matt.

"The Iron Horse was fading. Four hits in the four-game Yankee sweep. All singles. He could still hit, but the raw power was quickly being sapped from his body. By spring, his coordination would also be gone."

The threesome finished their late-afternoon walk in silence. There wasn't anything left to say. The Cubs had now lost the World Series six straight times dating back to 1910, including four in a recent ten-year span. And Lou Gehrig, thirty-five years old, was dying of a rare disease that would soon bear his name.

Matt and Jason bade farewell to their own Iron Horse at the entrance to the home and ambled to the nearby bus stop. Tiredness overwhelmed them as they walked. What they needed was a good nap.

CHAPTER 12

Mid-August saw the Cubs on a roll. The season's second half had begun with a sweep over Cincy, vaulting the North Siders over the Reds and back into second place. Since then, they had won with eerie regularity, the outstanding starting pitching reminiscent of the Sutcliffe-Trout-Eckersley-Sanderson tandem during the magical summer of '84. A lefty by the name of Holtzman had been called up from Triple-A Iowa to complement the staff's mainstays of Wood, Jenkins, and Brown. He was only nineteen, but he had amazed Sandberg and Girardi by hurling back-to-back no-hitters in his first two games in the Show. Thus, his unique, how-did-they-ever-come-up-with-it nickname: "No-No."

Baseball, more than any other sport, prided itself on nicknames. Walter Johnson, the Senators' legendary pitcher, was known as "The Big Train"; Ty Cobb was called the "Georgia Peach"; Ted Williams, "The Splendid Splinter"; Pete Rose, "Charlie Hustle"; Don Mattingly, "Donnie Baseball." There was "Blue Moon" Odom, "Catfish" Hunter, "Pee Wee" Reese, or Stan "The Man" Musial. And on and on throughout the decades. With a legacy such as this, the Cub faithful were positive the team couldn't lose with "Rusty," "Jolly," "Knuckles," and "No-No" manning the mound. The logic made perfect sense to rabid baseball fanatics whose team hadn't won the World Series since 1908.

However, Abner Doubleday Tripplehorn paid no attention to the nicknames. As the Cubs continued to excel, the old-timer was more and more convinced that the *surnames* were the real reason for hope.

****

Matthew Holmes and Jason Doyle, meanwhile, were caught up in the mounting anticipation of a glorious late-summer trip out East with their families. During the ten-day trip, they would visit Gettysburg, New York City—where Matt's father had wrangled tickets from a business partner to a Red Sox-Yankees game—and finally, Cooperstown, home of the Baseball Hall of Fame. When they returned home, only one week would remain before they entered the halls of Evanston Township High School. Only one week before their report on Abner would be due. It was decision time.

"It just might work. Besides, we have no other choice." Matt was laying out the arguments like a trained defense attorney trying to convince his client that the only way out was to accept a plea bargain and spend a reduced time locked away from society—possibly as few as twenty years.

Jason wasn't buying it. "It won't hold up."

"We have more than enough notes. All we need to do is visit Abner one more time for his take on the '45 Cubs, and we're done."

"And we get an F," scowled Jason.

"Not necessarily. Picture this. We title it: *Abner Tripplehorn and the Glory Years of the Chicago Cubs (1906-1945)*. Subtitle: *Forty Years of Baseball Bliss*."

"And we get an F," reiterated Jason.

"Not if we get Mr. McSherry for a teacher. I've heard he's really cool—a genuine sports junkie. He'll eat it up like Twinkies, and we'll get an A."

"And the odds are what—five-to-one? There are four other English teachers. What if we get Mrs. Peck? She's old school. She'll probably puke all over it and throw it back in our faces. Or we might each end up with a different English teacher. Then what? McSherry gives *you* an A, and old lady Peck gives *me* an F, that's what." Jason was starting to lose touch with reality.

"Not gonna happen. Don't you remember what Mrs. Hulbert said? Because of the special project, kids are assured of being paired with their partners in English classes."

"So, we strike out or hit a home run together?"

"Right. And I say, if we give it our best shot, we hit a homer."
Jason was still not convinced. "Maybe."

"Maybe," conceded Matt. "But, as I said before, we have no other choice. Abner's not going to come clean about his personal life. For all we know, he never even *had* a personal life. He's just the ultimate baseball fan, that's all."

Jason acquiesced. "Okay. Fine. But we might as well just turn in an essay titled: *Matthew Holmes, Jason Doyle, and the Suicidal Rage of the Postmodern Cubs Fan.*"

****

The goal was set: visit Abner one last time, get the scoop on the last Cubs N.L. pennant from one who saw it live, write the stupid report, and head off on the vacation of a lifetime.

"So, you start school soon?" Abby guided the boys through the maze of hallways, although by now it was all too familiar to them.

"Yes, we do."

"I'm sure you'll both do well. Just don't let those gorgeous girls distract you from your studies."

That would be a shame, thought the boys.

Upon reaching Room 101, they found Abner studying documents laid out before him on his desk. A CD of Abbott and Costello's "Who's on First?" played in the background.

"Hello, boys. Rest your tired fannies on the bed. I'll be with you in a minute."

"What're you up to, Abner?" asked Abby in her usual cheerful voice.

"Not much, Abs. Just writing you out of my will."

Abby smiled. "Oh, what a shame. I was so looking forward to that dollar and a quarter. Just as well. Now I won't have to pay the taxes on it. See you all later."

Abner continued to concentrate on the papers. At one point, he held one of the documents up where Matt and Jason could clearly see the heading: LAST WILL AND TESTAMENT. Perhaps Abner's throwaway line to Abby had been sincere.

It wasn't long before the boys were stifling their laughter in an attempt to give Abner some peace and quiet. Not easy when confronted with the crown jewel of comedy routines. (One didn't even have to be a baseball fan to love it.)

Abner made a few notations on the will, tucked it away in a large envelope, and turned to face his guests. "Haven't you ever heard this before?"

"Of course," said Jason defensively. "But it's funny every time."

"Can't argue with you there."

For the next several minutes, the room shook with unrestrained laughter as Bud and Lou, with perfect comic timing, finished the bit.

Abner ejected the CD and placed it carefully back in its case. The cover read: "Baseball's Greatest Hits."

"So, what's up?"

"We came to tell you we're going on vacation with our families," explained Matt. "To Cooperstown."

Abner's face brightened. "I take it you've never been there before?"

"No."

"You'll love it. Every fan should make the pilgrimage once in his lifetime."

"We're pumped," said Jason.

"As well you should be. Hey, do me a favor, will ya?" Abner reached into his wallet and extracted a five. "Buy me a postcard of Ron Santo's plaque. You'll see. The gift shop has cards of all the players' plaques."

Matt held up his hand, refusing the bill. "We can't take that, sir. This one's on us."

Abner withdrew the proffered money. "Why, thank you. I'll graciously accept the gift when you return. How long you gonna be gone?"

"About ten days," answered Jason. "We're visiting Gettysburg and New York City first."

"My grandfather was a Union soldier at Gettysburg. I'll have to tell you about it sometime."

Sirens and bells sounded in the boys' brains. This was the very narrative they had spent their summer trying to pry out of Abner. Farewell, Cubs; hello, real American history. The revised essay title shone like a spotlight in their eyes: *Grandfather Tripplehorn's Heroics at the Battle of Gettysburg*. They had struck gold.

"Mr. Abner, sir," asked Matt, "could you please tell us about it now?"

"Ain't much to tell. Amos Horatio Tripplehorn, my father's father, ran away from home at sixteen to join the fight. Lied about his age. First day at Gettysburg, guns were going off all o'er the place. He was scared right down to his socks, I reckon, so he decided to hightail it outta there. While he was running away, he tripped over a tree stump and broke his ankle. He never fired a shot. They sent him home with full military honors. Leastways that's how the story was passed down to me."

Matt and Jason experienced that sudden sinking feeling, like Cubs fans everywhere when Brant Brown dropped the routine fly ball in Milwaukee back in '98. It *should* have been caught; Abner's grandfather *should* have been a hero at Gettysburg; the boys *should* have chosen Oprah to interview.

"Anything else you youngsters want to know about the Civil War—other than what you learned in eighth-grade U.S. History, that is?"

Jason momentarily sprang to life. "What else can you tell us?"

"Nothin'. I wasn't there. Before my time. I can recommend some good books though."

The boys exhaled sighs of total defeat. It was back to square one.

Matt spoke up. "Could you tell us about the 1945 World Series then?"

"I was there for that, so, yes, I can." Abner reached into a bag atop his desk and pulled out a fistful of fun-size candy bars. "Care for a Twix?"

The summer that had begun with so much promise was coming to a close. Matt and Jason had enjoyed meeting Abner and spending time with him. But now the vacation beckoned, and they just wanted to get one last interview over with and go home.

"It was the end of World War II," began Abner in the timeless manner of an experienced storyteller. "Hard to believe, isn't it? The last time the Cubs played in the World Series was the same year we dropped the A-bomb on Japan. Most of the teams were missing their big stars. They had all either enlisted or been drafted. But early on, FDR proclaimed the games would go on, seeing as baseball was so important to the overall morale of the country.

"The Cubs battled the Cards for the pennant, took it, and then faced the Tigers for the fourth time in the Series. You may recall the heartbreaking loss to Detroit ten years earlier.

"Due to restrictions on wartime travel—even though the actual conflict was over by then—they used a 3-4 schedule for the games instead of the usual 2-3-2 set-up. The first three games were to be played in Detroit, the last four in Chicago.

"Legend has it that Stan Hack checked out third base before Game 1 to see if he was still stranded there ten years after the fact. He wasn't."

It was a funny anecdote, the punch line delivered in Abner's usual dry-as-a-bone style. The boys weren't sure if they should laugh or cry.

"Hank Borowy, obtained from the Yankees in mid-season, won Game 1 for Chicago by the lopsided score of 9-0. But slugger Hank Greenberg was back from overseas and itchin' to hit against the Cubs—you may remember he broke his wrist and missed the bulk of the '35 Series. His homer clinched Game 2 for Detroit, but the Cubs took Game 3 and headed back to Chi-town with a two games to one lead. They only had to split the last four to win."

It seemed the boys had heard this worn record too many times. Matt's grandfather had often bemoaned the infamous collapse of '69 when the Cubs all but had it in the bag. Jason's father had recalled his excitement as a five-year-old boy looking ahead to that "just one more win" when the '84 team boarded the plane for the fateful three-game series in San Diego.

And Matt's father had recently made mention of the 2003 NLCS Game 6 meltdown from his never-too-old-to-cry adult perspective. Why was it that, when Dame Fortune reached her arms out to embrace this particular baseball club, the manager and players ran from her like Abner's grandfather fleeing the Army of Northern Virginia? It almost seemed as if some terrible curse hung over the Cubs.

"Game 4." Abner's voice cut through the descending gloom. "Local tavern owner Billy Sianis brought his pet goat to the game. Patrons complained, and the goat was ejected. The crazy Greek put a hex on the team: no more World Series victories for the Cubs. Detroit promptly won Games 4 and 5.

"We attended Game 6. Sat in the right-field bleachers. The Cubs blew a big lead in the eighth when the Tigers scored four runs to tie it. Manager Charlie Grimm then called on his ace to hold 'em—even though Borowy had started and lost Game 5 the day before. Amazingly, he did just that. For the next four innings. The Cubs won on a two-out, bad-hop double in the bottom of the twelfth. It was the last World Series game our Cubs ever won."

As he had done many times, Abner used his 2020 time machine—bigger, better, bolder than H. G. Wells ever dreamed of—to transport all of them back to a time when America was in the midst of the celebration to end all celebrations. When a new generation of twenty-year-old boys who had been fortunate enough to come back alive was on the verge of leading the nation out of the darkness of its past sins and into the light of an ever-brightening future—as bright as the brightest sun in the brightest sky. The torch had indeed been passed.

"Game 7 was played two days later. Grimm wanted to win so badly he started Borowy again. It was a classic 'dance with the one who brung ya' move. But ole Hank was plumb wore out. The Tigers scored five in the first and never looked back. They won 9-3. The goat had the last laugh, and he's been laughin' ever since."

And then Abner spoke the truest words he had ever spoken to his new friends. "It was the saddest day of my life."

Matt and Jason exchanged perplexed looks.

"Were you at the game?" asked Matt.

Abner stiffened. His face turned ashen. His eyes shifted to the carpet, and he seemed to be on the brink of tears. When he looked back up at the boys, his eyes wet, the old man looked every bit the one hundred twenty years that he had lived. His voice came as if from the grave, far away and deathly somber. "No. I couldn't make it that day. I had somewhere else to be."

After a brief pause, Abner composed himself and said in a curt manner, "I think you'd better go now."

CHAPTER 13

"What was that all about?" asked Jason. The bus was crowded, and the boys stood in the aisle, jostling for space with other weary passengers.

"I haven't the foggiest," replied Matt, still reeling from Abner's rude dismissal. "But I know one thing for sure. Whatever it was, it didn't have anything to do with the Game 7 loss."

"Maybe we should ask Abby."

"Maybe. But for now let's just make sure we finish the report before we leave."

****

There was, of course, plenty of time to finish the essay prior to vacation. But procrastination has always been a way of life for most teens, especially when it comes to homework, and Matt and Jason were no exception. So, when the minivan pulled out of Matt's driveway on a clear, sun-drenched morning, the revised plan was to complete it upon their return. After all, they would have an entire week before school started.

"You two finish that report yet?" Mr. Holmes' voice came from the driver's seat. The seating arrangement inside the van was as follows: Mrs. Holmes rode shotgun beside her husband; Mr. and Mrs. Doyle sat in captain's chairs behind them; Matt's ten-year-old sister Joy shared the bench seat in back with the two boys.

"Almost." Technically, this was not a lie. Ninety percent of the work—the research—was in the bag. A quick typing job was all that remained.

"You should have finished it by now."

"Your father's right."

Matt rolled his eyes, fervently hoping that, by the time the minivan rolled through Indiana and into Ohio, the subject would be changed.

"Daddy, Matt rolled his eyes!"

"Don't roll your eyes, Matt," admonished Mrs. Holmes.

These first few minutes of the trip proved the indisputable fact that there was no such thing as a unique family vacation by car. Each was the same as the next. Siblings fought over an inch of space, the last package of fruit snacks, or which DVD to play—earlier generations of kids fought over which radio station to play. (Pioneer children crossing the Great Plains in covered wagons probably fought over what songs to sing.) Parents argued over the number of stops per day for food or bathroom breaks versus the concept of "making good time," a mostly male philosophy.

That this was a combined Holmes-Doyle vacation did little to increase harmony or relieve stress:

"Does your husband snore that loud all the time?"

"I know it's only been an hour since the last stop, but I really have to go!"

"Mommy, Matt took my magazine and won't give it back!"

****

A person's first visit to the battlefields of Gettysburg was not likely to be forgotten. That this peaceful landscape had once exploded in horrific violence—51,000 American casualties in only three days—was inconceivable. Had that much human blood soaked the ground? Had a place ever been more appropriately named than Devil's Den? Had the failure of Pickett's Charge on the third day been the Civil War's turning point?

The more the two families learned about the epic battle from their tour guide, the more somber they became. The details picked up would surely help Joy when her fifth-grade class studied U.S. History in the coming school year. And although

Matt and Jason *thought* they knew what happened here in 1863, their emotions were caught off guard by the magnitude of the carnage.

"And one of the Union Army's heroes on the first day of fighting," intoned their guide, "was Major General Abner Doubleday."

Upon hearing the familiar name, both boys' senses were alerted.

"As some of you probably know, Abner Doubleday was once given credit for having invented the American version of baseball, in 1839, in Cooperstown, New York. Today, historians dispute this claim as there are few, if any, hard facts to back it up.

"True or not, however, one thing cannot be argued— Doubleday's bravery on the first day of battle was his finest hour."

The docent went on to tell the story of how Doubleday's 9,500 men had held off 16,000 Confederates, causing heavy losses among the enemy's ranks until overpowered by the sheer numbers and forced to retreat.

Matt and Jason couldn't help but wonder if Amos Horatio Tripplehorn's fearful flight had been the catalyst for panic among the Union troops.

In the end, they learned that Doubleday had been shot in the neck on the second day but survived. Overall, he had been a courageous leader in the "War Between the States," the guide informed them, and a statue had been erected at Gettysburg in honor of his gallant service.

The boys' conclusion about the man for whom their friend had been named? Did he invent the game of baseball? Probably not. Did it matter? Not in the least.

****

It wasn't the "House That Ruth Built." *That* Yankee Stadium—opened in 1923 and renovated in the mid-1970s— had been razed in favor of its twenty-first century offspring.

87

Now a decade old, the newer model sat sleek and polished like a just-off-the-assembly-line car. But although the Yankees continued to win, the new edifice couldn't hold a candle to the old palace and the history-making events—including baseball, football, and boxing—that were once proudly showcased there.

Several attempts had been made, however, to incorporate the Yankees' glorious past into the new stadium, including the mirroring of the old stadium's exterior, the replicating of the frieze along the roof of the upper-deck stands, and the relocation of Monument Park. Located beyond center field, this park was created to display retired uniform numbers, plaques, and monuments dedicated to ordinary men who had been transformed into legends dressed in the dark blue pinstripes of the most famous franchise in sports history.

Baseball fans from around the country were left breathless at the sight of so much greatness representing one team. Matt and Jason stood spellbound with their fathers, all the while thinking what Abner would say—what stories he'd tell—if he was there. Probably regale them with a tale about how he had challenged the Babe to a pancake-eating contest—and won.

Their seats were tucked away in the right-field corner, a potentially good place to catch a long foul ball, but not a very good spot to see much of the game. But that didn't matter much to Matt and Jason. They were here to watch a duel between the Yanks and Red Sox, the pinnacle of baseball contests.

In New York in the 1950s, the Dodgers and Giants fought each other like barbarians; high spikes and inside fastballs a run-of-the-mill approach to their warfare. As fans used to say, Giants pitcher Sal "The Barber" Maglie didn't get his nickname from his part-time job. When the bitter rivals moved to Los Angeles and San Francisco respectively, the enmity traveled west with them. Giants pitcher Juan Marichal even introduced Dodgers catcher John Roseboro to his bat—"Say hello to my little friend"—in one of the most chilling incidents in baseball history. Nor was there any love lost between the Cubs and Cardinals in the heart of the Midwest. But Yankees versus Red Sox gave a whole new meaning to the term: 'til death do us part.

From back in the early twentieth century, when the Boston Pilgrims faced off against the New York Highlanders, there was just something these two teams—and their rabid fans—disliked about each other. The lowly Irish and Italian immigrants seemed to always be looking up at those snobby New Yorkers. In fact, professional baseball was the only way the Boston fans could trump those obnoxious metropolitans in the beginning, the mighty Red Sox winning five of the first fifteen World Series.

Then, the Babe was sold, Yankee Stadium was built, and twenty-six World Championships followed before Boston won another one. Each successive title was a slap in the face to the Boston faithful, who suffered under the Curse of the Bambino for eighty-six miserable years. Since 2004, when the Red Sox "reversed the curse," only Chicago baseball fans have known this depth of suffering. (The Chicago White Sox reversed their own eighty-eight-year curse in 2005, referred to simply as the "stupid-is-as-stupid-does" curse in honor of the Black Sox Scandal of 1919, a scant two years after their last title in 1917.)

Matt, Jason, and their dads watched as neutral observers, hoping for a close contest while munching on nachos and sipping on sodas. Matt kept meticulous score so as to be able to show Abner when they got back home. Outs were made; runs were scored; and ghosts of bygone seasons flitted back-and-forth across the diamond, baseball's past melding in perfect unison with its present.

"I hope the girls are having a good time," remarked Mr. Holmes.

"On a shopping spree in New York City?" offered Mr. Doyle. "Are you kidding? Of course, they are."

The game moved along. The start of the eighth inning saw the teams tied at 4-4.

"Let's go get some ice cream," said Matt, turning to his friend.

Jason, always eager for food, readily agreed.

"Hey, Dad," said Matt, shoving his scorecard into his father's hand, "we're going for ice cream. Keep score for me, will ya?"

"Sure," came the answer. "Be careful now. Don't get lost."

Matt thought there was no way that could happen. All ballparks, despite their idiosyncrasies, were essentially the same. And he was right about that. But there were other ways he never imagined that he could be thrown for a loop.

Having secured their waffle cones, the boys made their way through the crowd back toward their seats. Glancing down at the field boxes, Matt gave a sudden start.

"Look!" He grabbed Jason by the arm. "Down there! In the rich-people seats! Do you see what I see?"

Jason looked.

There could be no mistake. Walking along, cane in one hand and beer in the other, was—

"Abner!" yelled Jason. "Holy Cow! What's he doing here?"

Abner Doubleday Tripplehorn took his seat behind the first-base dugout. He was not alone. His companion, who greeted him with an affectionate peck on the cheek, was an attractive older woman dressed in a neat pants suit.

"Let's go!" shouted Matt as he headed down the aisle with Jason right behind.

Two steps later, their progress was halted by a burly security guard in the guise of a friendly usher. "Sorry, boys, but unless you have tickets, you can't go down into those seats."

"But we know that guy!" pleaded Jason, pointing toward the luxury boxes.

"Sure you do," said the usher, flashing a fierce grin. "And I know the pope. But you're still not goin' down there without a ticket."

"Please, sir," begged Matt, "this is very important. That man is our good friend. He's one hundred twenty years old, and he's with the blond."

The usher, trained hunter that he was, spotted Abner's silver hair in the sunshine below. The old gentleman was leaning over and whispering something in his date's ear. She laughed in response.

"Quite a pair, huh?" The usher's voice dripped with sarcasm. "Who knows, maybe it's Joe DiMaggio and Marilyn Monroe back from the dead to put a new curse on the Sox?"

The man's supernatural explanation, the boys thought, was just as credible as Abner showing up in New York at the same game they were attending. They must be mistaken. It just looked like him. Still . . .

"Excuse me, but the hoax is over. Either you head on back to your seats, or I escort you out the gates. What's it gonna be?"

It was no use. If it really was Abner, they weren't going to get to visit him today. Dejectedly, they turned away from the psychopathic Lurch-a-like and dragged themselves back to their seats, the waffle cones leaking in the heat.

"What took you guys so long?"

"Long line," muttered Matt.

Over the next few innings—the Yankees finally won on a throwing error in the bottom of the twelfth—the boys ruminated over what they were sure they had seen. How had Abner gotten to New York? Was he a runaway? And who was the mystery blond?

After another day of sightseeing—Central Park, the Statue of Liberty, and the Empire State Building all lived up to their reputations—the two families left for Cooperstown. Here, in the quaint village where James Fenimore Cooper, author of *The Last of the Mohicans*, lived and wrote, Matt and Jason would receive, as if from above, the answer to all their questions—and more.

CHAPTER 14

One can't *get* to Cooperstown unless one *goes* to Cooperstown. It's not on the way to or from anywhere. The last twisting, turning twenty miles might just be some of upstate New York's most beautiful wilderness. And the town itself is a whole lot less touristy than one would expect. Most significantly, for baseball fans, it is Heaven on Earth.

Matt, Jason, and their families sat on shade-shrouded benches awaiting the morning's opening of the Hall of Fame. The boys shot curious glances in every direction, half expecting Abner to waltz into the scene at any moment. "Well, hello there, boys! Sorta thought I'd find you here." And why not? He had stalked them at Yankee Stadium, hadn't he? Or had he?

All thoughts of a cloak-and-dagger Abner were pushed out of their minds when baseball's Pearly Gates swung open. For the next few hours, Matt and Jason hung out with the immortals. Or at least with their graven images. The museum showcased relics from seasons past, each display echoing some great achievement or event. There were: bats, balls, gloves, spikes, and similar paraphernalia that had played a part in the ongoing drama called baseball.

There were photos too. Abner's stories came to life in black-and-white images of "Three-Finger" Brown, Fred Merkle, and the Polo Grounds. There was Babe Ruth the pitcher and Babe Ruth the hitter. There was Connie Mack, resplendent in white suit and straw hat, like a general with a secret "Mack Attack" up his sleeve. And there was a grinning Gabby Hartnett stepping on home plate to celebrate the Homer in the Gloamin'.

Abner had introduced the boys to a small part of baseball history—an appetizer to stimulate their hunger. Here sat the smorgasbord. The Negro Leagues and their superstars were no longer concealed in the dark shadow of racism. And the All-American Girls Professional Baseball League shone brightly in the light of the significant role it played during World War II, when ballplayers traded pinstripes for a different type of uniform.

Matt announced at the day's end, "I've never seen so much cool stuff in my life."

No one disagreed with his assessment.

****

"Let's see what's on," said Jason. As worn out as they were from their journey through baseball-land, the boys were never too tired to watch television. They collapsed into the comfy lounge chairs in the lobby of the bed-and-breakfast where they were staying. Matt snatched up the remote from the glass cocktail table in front of them and punched the power button.

The picture popped on, bright and clear. The boys froze. Had the giant screen projected an image of California falling into the Pacific Ocean, Matt and Jason could not have been more thoroughly shocked.

Sitting in a rocking chair and wearing a coat and tie, their friend Abner smiled out at a nation of viewers. The mystery blond sat across from him. In retrospect, it seemed odd that the boys hadn't recognized her at the ballpark. Now ninety—and as charming and attractive as ever—Barbara Walters began her interview. For the next twenty minutes, Matt and Jason sat motionless, listening to what might have been, with a little luck, *their* interview.

****

Barbara: "Good evening, viewers. I'm Barbara Walters. I'd like to introduce you to my first guest for tonight's show, Abner Doubleday Tripplehorn. Believe it or not, Mr. Tripplehorn was born in the year 1900. That makes him exactly one hundred twenty years old. As far as we know, he is the world's oldest living human being, and he's here to share with us some of the experiences he's had during his long life." (Turning to face her guest.) "Why don't we start with your early years? What do you most remember about your first twenty years, Mr. Tripplehorn?"

Abner: "Please, Barbara, call me Abner. Well, the first fifteen years were rather uneventful. And then came that horrible boating excursion."

Barbara: "Would you tell us about that?"

Abner: "July 24, 1915. My father was working for Western Electric in Chicago then. The company had rented a few cruise boats to whisk all the employees and their families across Lake Michigan to the other side for a picnic. We all boarded at the Clark Street loading dock right there in the Chicago River— carefree, excited families looking forward to a day of sun and fun. The boat was still tied up to the dock when it capsized. My father and mother were down below. I was up on deck looking for my aunt and uncle—my father's brother. They were supposed to join up with us. So, when the boat tipped over, I was thrown into the water and survived. My parents, trapped in the boat's interior, weren't so fortunate. You can look it up, Barbara. The Eastland disaster took the lives of 844 passengers, more *passengers* than those who perished on the Titanic, plus a handful of the crew. Yet most people have never heard of it. Obviously, it was a turning point in my life as I, an only child, was suddenly an orphan."

Barbara: "How awful that must have been for you. How did you go on?"

Abner: "It wasn't easy. My Aunt Vivian and Uncle Gregg arrived late that fateful day. They were still on the dock when the boat flipped. After the funerals, they took me in and raised me. They didn't have any children of their own, so I think it helped them in a way. They were very good to me. You know, Barbara, the one thing I took away from that terrible day was that there were no guarantees in life, just hope. Hope for a better future. So, I set out to make one for myself as best I could. I don't know if I ever would have made it if my darling Vera hadn't come along."

Barbara: "Your wife?"

Abner: "She was. Not initially, of course. Christmas, 1917, brought us together. My folks had been gone for over two years. I was struggling in school. Never was a very good student, and after the tragedy, well . . . I tailed off even more. Uncle Gregg said I needed to get a part-time job to help with the upcoming holidays, so I showed up at Marshall Field's on State Street and applied for work as a stock boy. Didn't know it then, but a pretty young thing about my age was already working in the gift department—wrapping Christmas presents for the customers. We met my first day on the job—in the break room."

Barbara: "Let me guess. She spotted your handsome face when you walked in?"

Abner: "Hardly. I didn't clean up so well in those days, even in a brand new white shirt. She most likely wouldn't have even noticed me if I hadn't knocked over a cup of coffee that spilled off the counter and onto the floor. A veteran stock boy sneered at me as if I'd shot his dog and warned me that, if I handled the merchandise in such a careless fashion, I wouldn't last a week. As you can imagine, Barbara, I was mortified. But all that changed when, down on my hands and knees, I looked up into the sweetest pair of eyes I'd ever seen. Her kind nature had overcome her, and she'd hurried to help the clumsy new boy clean up the mess."

Barbara: "I'm not sure, Abner, but that sounds like love at first sight. Was it?"

Abner: "It was for me. I was so head over heels, I went out and busted an entire box of Christmas dishes that same day. Luckily for me, the manager liked me—I'm not sure why—and kept me on even after the holidays. During the next year, Vera and I worked in various departments as the need arose, but we always seemed to end up together in that break room. It didn't take long for real communication to develop between us. I liked to talk; she liked to listen. I saved up to buy her Frango Mints for her birthday; she brought me home to meet her folks. We were married in their apartment on April 30, 1919, a week after she turned eighteen. We never left Field's. Ended up working there until we retired—her behind the jewelry counter, me in men's clothing."

Barbara: "Did you have any children?"

Abner: "One son. Francis. He was born in 1923, four years into our marriage. We were still living with Vera's parents then, which helped because she didn't have to quit her job. Field's was real nice about her getting some time off. No maternity leave back then. Our Francis grew up to be a fine boy. Distinguished himself in the Battle of the Bulge during World War II. Anyway, we finally got our own apartment in '24. Uncle Gregg had used the relief money from the tragedy to buy a few small apartments on the North Side. He was a great landlord—took care of all his tenants well. Vera and I ended up living in one rent free. I helped out fixing things as part of our agreement. You know, painting, plumbing, electrical work, whatever came up. I got to be quite handy after awhile."

Barbara: "You seem like such an optimistic person, Abner. What keeps you going after so many years?"

Abner: "Well, Barbara, I guess you could say I'm always interested in what comes next. No matter how much a person learns from experiences, it seems like there's always something up around the bend. For example, Vera and I had twenty-five wonderful years of retirement together before she passed, and early on, while we were both in our seventies, we decided to see the world. We'd saved up money through our working years. So, we set off on our trip in the spring of '75. Came home that fall so we wouldn't miss the Bicentennial celebration the following year."

Barbara: "Where did you travel?"

Abner: "Why, just about everywhere. Started out in England, where our kin come from. Met the Queen—she was a real sweetie. Then, from there, we followed our hearts. Kissed the Blarney Stone and climbed the Eiffel Tower. Entered the gates of the death camp at Auschwitz. Rode camels and stood in awe of the Egyptian Pyramids. Walked where Jesus walked—hard to explain that feeling. Spent the month of August touring Italy and Greece. Stopped by the Vatican and heard Pope Paul VI speak. Saw the sites of Rome, Naples, and Venice. Visited Athens— the Parthenon was indescribable. You can never get too much education about people and places, Barbara. Life is beautiful."

Barbara: "Yes, it is. I understand you now live in a very nice retirement community in Evanston, Illinois, just north of Chicago. How do you keep busy during the day?"

Abner: "Oh, I try to keep my mind active by reading, playing board games, and shooting pool with the other geezers."

Barbara: "Do you ever receive any visitors?"

Abner: "Well, Barbara, you've got to understand that most people who would normally visit me are too dead to bother— you know, my old friends from the glory days. Seems like I've gone and outlived them all. But I do have two new friends— nice young men named Matt and Jason. They come by every now and then to shoot the breeze. They'll be in high school soon, so I suppose they won't be coming around as often as they used to. Can't say I blame 'em. Sometimes I don't treat 'em as fair as I should. But they're good fellows, that's for sure."

Barbara: "Well, Abner, it's good to know you're still making friends. And now, I'm afraid it's time to end this segment of 'The Barbara Walters Special.' Please stay tuned for my next guest, fourteen-year-old fashion queen Suri Cruise, who will be with us following these brief commercial messages. And thank you, Abner, for sharing a small part of your life with us. Perhaps you will honor us with another visit ten years from now."

Abner: "Don't count me out, Barbara."

But Matt and Jason felt counted out. Out of a chance to have gained a true perspective of Abner's life—that he was not merely a half-crazed baseball fan, but that he was a courageous man who had survived against all odds when he had been orphaned at age fifteen, his parents the victims of one of the most infamous catastrophes of the last century. Plus, his courtship and marriage, his son fighting in the war, his world travels. These were interesting topics. These were topics that an English teacher would soak up like a bread-wielding diner attacking a plate full of leftover linguine sauce. But noooooooooooo. All they had for their report was a bunch of stories about a stupid baseball team that always came up short of the grand prize. And headaches. They had headaches.

CHAPTER 15

The long ride home through exotic cities such as Buffalo and Cleveland was a quiet one, especially for Matt and Jason. They spent the time staring out the dirty car windows and contemplating their future as high school inched closer with every passing hour. Perhaps they'd make a smooth adjustment; perhaps they wouldn't. But one thing could not be disputed. Abner had stiffed them. They had put their faith in him to give them the stories they needed for their report, and he had withheld them in order to woo Barbara Walters. These narratives, steeped in pathos, had tugged at the heartstrings. Abner's baseball stories, in contrast, left one ultimately unsatisfied, like building up hope and then leaving the bases loaded in the bottom of the ninth. The boys were quite convinced that any teacher reading them would fail to appreciate their merit. In other words, an F. They were doomed.

****

"Yes, this is Abigail Sweeney. Who's calling please?"

"Hi, Abby. It's Matt Holmes."

"Oh, hi, Matt. How was your vacation?"

"We had a great time." A half-truth.

"Good. I'm glad you enjoyed it. So, what can I do for you?"

"Is Abner back from New York yet?"

"So, you found out about his little jaunt, did you? I assume you saw the show."

"Oh, we saw it all right."

"He's quite the sly old fox. He even managed to keep it from me until the day before he left. By then, the details were all arranged. The flight, accommodations, everything—all paid for and supervised by ABC. The home insisted he couldn't fly alone, so we sent two novice nurses with him. He ditched them at JFK."

"Then he's not back yet?"

"No, Matt, he's not. NBC executives saw the interview and, not to be outdone by a rival network, booked him to host 'Saturday Night Live' this coming weekend. We assume he's coming back on Sunday, but anything's possible now that he's gotten a taste of the good life."

Great, thought Matt.

"Did you want to see him again?" asked Abby.

"We did. But it doesn't matter now. We have to turn in our report on Monday, so it's too late now to get any more info from him. We'll have to go with what we've got."

"I see," said a thoughtful Abby.

"Please tell Abner we said hi and thanks for everything. Thanks to you as well. Jason and I really appreciate what you've done for us."

"Perhaps there's one more thing I can do for you. We'll have to wait and see. Until then, good-bye and good luck to both of you."

Matt punched off his cell phone and relayed the gist of the conversation to Jason, who received the news glumly. "What did she mean by 'one more thing'?"

"I dunno."

"I know something," grinned Jason. "I wouldn't miss this week's 'SNL' for the world."

****

Trepidation ruled the week before the boys were to enter high school. They had, of course, heard the tales of terror regarding the hazing of freshmen on the first day, and they awoke in the night in sweat-soaked fear from dreadful dreams of such torture. Jason envisioned himself mummified in Saran Wrap, wandering out into a busy street in front of the school while trying to avoid being run over by swerving cars and buses.

Matt pictured himself locked in a glass showcase, staring out like a helpless mime while his new peers ridiculed his plight.

Daytime was dominated by endless trips to buy numerous school supplies: pens, pencils, spirals, assignment notebooks, and new backpacks to carry them all. Trendy clothes were all the rage, the better to appear not quite as geeky as first-day freshmen actually were. Area drugstores experienced a gold rush-like stampede on products such as deodorant, shaving cream, cologne, and dandruff shampoo as boys cast off their summer look—and smell—in favor of a more civilized approach to their new life.

To celebrate the end of summer, Matt and Jason made one last visit to Wrigley Field. It was a Wednesday afternoon game against the Giants, who led the West Division by two games over the Dodgers. The Cubs still held second in the Central, four games behind St. Louis. From their terrace seats on the third-base side, the boys witnessed something they had heard about (once) but had never seen.

In the top of the ninth with the score tied 1-1, the Giants had runners on the corners with two men out. "Booby" Bonds was at bat. (The nickname had come about after the slugger was caught using steroids and suspended for a full season. When he returned, he was hindered by massive man-breasts.) The count went to 0-2. On the next pitch, "Sober" Sutter's split-finger fastball failed to split, and "Booby" crushed a single up the middle. Hit so hard, it reached "Shorty" Wilson on one sizzling hop. The center fielder did not misplay this one. Rather, he fired a cannon shot on a line toward home while the runner was only halfway down the third-base line. The crowd, on its feet, uttered a collective gasp. There would be a play at the plate.

Baseball, it has been said, is a slow-paced game punctuated by sudden bursts of frenzied action. This was one such moment. In a split second, the ball short-hopped its way into "Squats" Hartnett's glove. He reached out to swipe-tag the runner's leg, whose spikes swept across home plate in an explosion of diamond dust.

"Safe!" bellowed the umpire.

The crowd booed lustily. In the twinkling of an eye, the game had changed dramatically. Had the call gone the other way, the third out would have been registered, the score would still be tied, and the Cubs would be coming to bat in the bottom of the ninth with a chance to score once and earn the victory. As it was, the Giants led 2-1, and nothing could change that now.

But wait . . . what was this? "Squats" was springing up from the ground and rifling the ball to "Hands" Herman, who was standing on second base and yelling to beat the band.

When everyone in the park had frozen seconds ago to watch the exciting play at home, "everyone" included Giants rookie Fred "the Elk" Elkrem. Leading off first base, he had broken quickly toward second at the crack of the bat. In fact, "the Elk," put in the game as a pinch runner solely because of his blinding speed, was so close to second when the line drive reached Wilson that "Shorty" had opted to throw home instead. But, in a that's-why-they-call-him-a-rookie moment, young Fred stopped in his tracks a step or two shy of second to turn and watch the play at the plate. He was still standing there when the ball smacked into Herman's glove for the convenient force and the third out.

When the Cubs claimed the contest on "Boom-Boom" Banks' long home run in the bottom of the ninth, the papers labeled Fred's brain freeze "Elkrem's Folly."

****

"Don't say it out loud," said Jason as the El train clattered along. "It'll jinx the team."

"Don't say what?" asked Matt, who knew perfectly well what.

"Don't say anything about that kid's mistake. It could happen to anybody at anytime."

"Yeah, assuming that anytime is once every century or so."

Jason frowned. "What d'ya think you-know-who will think about it?"

"You mean Abner?"

"No names, please."

"I think he'll not be a bit surprised." Matt turned to look at Jason with a combination of fear and awe. "I think, somehow, he has known all along it would happen like this."

****

"Live from New York, it's Saturday Night!" But this wasn't just any "SNL" broadcast. This was the kick-off to the new television season, scheduled to begin for all the networks in a few weeks. NBC was jumping the gun for this special presentation, just as Barbara Walters had done for ABC. The show was to be a celebration of the forty-fifth anniversary of its groundbreaking venture that had caught the nation by surprise with its sketch humor based on what was happening now. In its inaugural season, Chevy Chase, Gilda Radner, Jane Curtain, John Belushi, Dan Aykroyd, Laraine Newman, and Garrett Morris captured the hearts of the baby boomers and set the irreverent tone for a half-century of cutting-edge antics. The living members of the original cast—along with Bill Murray and Steve Martin—had been invited back for the party. And a party it was.

By the time the rehearsals were finished, the cast members were fatigued from a string of late nights on the town— behaving as if they were still in their twenties (and Abner still in his seventies). When the show opened, Abner's role was easy: warm up the audience. Wearing Steve Martin's trademark "arrow-through-the-head" prop, the old gentleman—dressed in tux and tails—split the sides of the viewers with one-liners from the golden age of comedy, borrowing from the vast repertoires of Hope, Benny, and Burns.

The skits featured the Not Ready For Prime Time Players reprising their greatest hits from the show's early days, from the Land Shark to the Cone Heads to the Samurai Delicatessen, with a surprisingly agile Abner performing Belushi's role in the latter. He also filled in for the late comedian in an update of The Thing That Wouldn't Leave and paired up with Aykroyd as the new and improved Blues Brothers. The after-party saw him fending off paparazzi as he danced the night away with the Kardashian sisters.

Airborne for O'Hare the next day, Abner Doubleday Tripplehorn had achieved a brand-new status as America's newest celebrity.

****

The Evanston Public Library was quiet on most Sunday evenings. This one was no exception. Earlier in the weekend, students searching for summer-reading books had surged into the stacks, vowing to never again wait until the last minute to complete their ten-week assignment. Sophomores, juniors, and seniors begged indifferent librarians to find that one misplaced copy of *Hamlet* or *A Man For All Seasons*, to no avail. Would Red Box have copies of the old movies in their "classics" section?

Trapped in a numbing melancholy, Matt and Jason sat at the computer and typed their report on Abner's life as a baseball fan. Make that a committed baseball fan. He *should* be committed, they thought. He could entertain the patients with his songs and stories.

"Finished," said Matt as the final word was typed.

Jason, seated beside his friend, peered at the paper. The last line read: "And since that sad day in October of 1945, the Chicago Cubs have never played in another World Series."

Exhausted, they thought they could almost hear Abner saying, "It was the saddest day of my life."

Matt went to hit print and paused.

"Perhaps you'd like to hear why it was so sad." This time Abner's voice did not come to them in a faraway haze. This time it was close and clear.

Matt and Jason turned around to see Abner looking over their shoulders. Abby stood beside him.

"What are you doing here?" asked Jason.

"Well," said Abner, "you may recall that, the last time we were together, I dismissed you rather summarily. First, I'd like to apologize for that. I hope you'll forgive me. Second, I'd like to fill in the blanks, so to speak, on the last game of the 1945 World Series. I believe there were some important details I neglected to share with you. Details about my personal life. Abs convinced me it was the right thing to do. She suggested I may have let you boys down, and I never meant to do that. So, if we could all be seated at this nice table over here, I want to tell you a story."

CHAPTER 16

The first week of high school flew by, and by Friday, Matt and Jason felt as if they'd been there forever. If anything, it seemed easier than they'd expected. There was little work. Most of their time was spent on various types of orientation—all-school assembly to become acquainted with the school rules; library "look-around"; meet-the-sponsors sign-up for extra-curricular activities. And the teachers were nice too. Each covered his or her syllabus and class procedures, checked out books, and gave only minor homework assignments to help break in the freshmen. Mrs. Peck, contrary to slanderous rumor, was exceptionally kind, promising her students a fun-filled year of learning with reading, writing, and speaking all incorporated into English 1.

The first weekend spilled over into Labor Day, and the gray-haired lady promised she would return the summer essays—critiqued and graded—on "Tuesday next," which her classes astutely interpreted to mean "next Tuesday." Matt and Jason had scratched out a last-minute revision, focusing *not* on the historical significance of the Cubs' ten pennants in forty years but on the personal significance—for one of their oldest fans—of the final two games of the team's last visit to the World Series seventy-five years ago.

Labor Day always signaled the stretch drive for Major League Baseball—a line of demarcation for who's in and who's out of each year's pennant races. Of course, 2020 was different due to the three-week extension of the regular season well into October. Teams within ten or twelve games of first place refrained from bringing up promising rookies, correctly assuming they were still in the hunt—at least for a wild-card spot.

The Cubs were in a good position, four games behind the Cardinals and four games ahead of the pesky Reds. As Monday dawned, preparing for an afternoon contest in Pittsburgh, they also found themselves only three games behind the Phillies and the Padres, who were tied for the two N.L. wild-card openings. The finish was shaping up to be an exciting one.

It had been an exciting week at Serenity Now Retirement Community as well. The media swarmed like sharks for a sound bite from Abner, who had hired an agent—one "Moonshine" Mulligan, another resident of the home—to handle his rapidly expanding business affairs. In his career, "Moonshine" had been a mid-level talent agent, and he knew a good thing when he saw it. After all, Abner's wealth was suddenly on the upswing. Already, he was booked for a September appearance on "The Tonight Show Starring Chris Rock," and *People* magazine had descended upon the home for the photo shoot of their annual edition titled "World's Sexiest Man."

Monday morning found Abner up early, shuffling through his drawers to find just the right tie for his ten o'clock meeting with the top brass at McDonald's headquarters, where he was being signed for a series of commercials celebrating the franchise's sixty-fifth anniversary. The crafty ad men were poised to somehow link Abner's longevity to his love of Big Macs and Quarter Pounders. That Abner had eaten at the fast-food giant only twice in his life was deemed irrelevant, and "Moonshine" urged his client to sign on the dotted line and gladly pocketed his ten percent fee.

By one in the afternoon, the tired old man was tucked away in his room watching the Cubs pound on the Pirates 14-3. "Stretch" Williams hit three homers and drove in seven, but Abner ended up missing the bulk of the scoring, opting instead for a two-hour nap. He awoke at three feeling refreshed and alert.

Abby rapped twice on the door and entered. "Did you have a nice nap?"

"Saw every pitch. And, by the way, didn't anybody ever teach you to knock before you barge into a gentleman's quarters? What if I'd been in a state of undress?"

"Nothing I haven't seen before. No big thrill. And I did knock—twice. Your hearing must be going."

"Hmmmf," grunted Abner.

"Time to freshen up. Your visitors will be here soon."

"Absolutely not. I told you before, Abs, I'm plumb tuckered out from all the hullabaloo this past week. Today is Labor Day, and I'm resting from my labor. What's for dinner tonight?"

"These aren't business visitors," Abby shot back. "These are friends. Matt and Jason are stopping by to say hi. And—if I may be allowed to comment—I think it's quite kind of them to give up some of their holiday to spend time with a cranky old codger like you."

For once, Abner had no retort. He knew that the boys had accomplished the task that had led them to call on him in the first place, and he was inwardly delighted that they cared enough for him to visit after the report had been turned in.

"Well, I suppose that's okay then. When will they be here?"

"Soon. You should change your shirt. It's got ketchup down the front."

"Yeah. That's from my McDonald's meeting this morning. I never ate so many fries."

✶✶✶✶✶✶✶✶✶✶✶✶✶✶✶✶

Matt and Jason had debated visiting Abner. Now that he was famous—one of his dances with Kim Kardashian had gone viral on YouTube—he might be too busy to talk to them. But they desperately wanted to seek his opinion on the Cubs' chances as August slipped into cool September. Could they catch the Cardinals?

"Maybe. Maybe not," said Abner.

The three amigos were sitting in the garden where they had first met. Abner had welcomed them and even encouraged them to ask questions about the unfolding pennant race. For him, it was comforting to have somebody who loved baseball to talk to again.

"You see," expounded Abner, "in some ways, the Cubs are in the best position. If they finish second, everyone will say they just didn't have the horses to catch St. Louis. If they win the division, everyone will applaud their come-from-behind rally while, at the same time, accusing the Cardinals of choking."

"So," said Jason, "did the '69 Cubs choke, or were the Mets just a better team?"

"You raise an interesting question, son. And you can bet your bottom dollar that no one knows the answer. Oh, there's been some high and mighty speculation on that subject for fifty years now, but I don't think anyone will ever figure out why the Mets won and the Cubs lost. I can tell you one thing though. It's impossible to find another team in the history of Chicago sports as beloved as the '69 Cubs."

"Why is that?" asked Matt.

"Hard to say. I guess it's because they gave the city one of the most thrilling summers ever. Forget that four of their Opening Day starters would eventually be enshrined in the Hall of Fame. Forget that the stars would all eventually retire or be traded having never won an N.L. pennant. Forget the torment of September after being in first place for 155 consecutive days. Remember only—if you were lucky enough to have been around back then—the absolute magic of that summer for the fans, the players, the media, everyone. It was like *Romeo and Juliet*, a great love affair that happened to have a bitter ending."

"My grandfather says the Cubs were exhausted by September because the manager played the same guys every day," said Matt.

"True as rain," agreed Abner. "They were physically exhausted from all those day games at Wrigley during a very hot summer—remember, no lights yet. And they were mentally exhausted from all the distractions of being celebrities—TV and radio spots endorsing every product imaginable, public appearances, etcetera, etcetera, etcetera. None of the players had ever experienced that kind of round-the-clock attention. It can wear on a fellow."

Had Abner been listening to himself, he might have detected the irony in his last statement.

"So, how did it happen?" asked Jason.

"It just did, that's how. It's easier to pinpoint *when*. September 3rd through September 15th. The Cubs lost eleven of twelve. The Mets won twelve of fifteen. Don't need to be a math wiz to figure what it meant. That was the season."

The boys slumped in their seats, wounded by the painful past.

"My wife and I were recently retired then, so we took in a lot of games that summer. Only sat with the bleacher bums once though. They were crude. Constantly yelling at the visiting outfielders about where and with whom the players had spent the night. No place for a lady, and my Vera was a lady.

"We were there on September 7th—hey, that's today, isn't it?—when Willie Stargell hit the home run off Phil Regan with two out in the ninth to tie it. The Pirates went on to win it in extras and sweep the three-game series. I honestly believe the Cubs never recovered from that home run.

"The next two nights, in New York, they lost to the Mets. That's when someone let that black cat onto the field right in front of the Cubs' dugout, just like a Poe story. Leo Durocher—the manager—kept staring at it like it was a witch or a devil or something. I dunno, maybe it was. Remember, the Mets were an expansion team in 1962, had never finished higher than ninth in a ten-team league, had been nine and a half games behind the Cubs in mid-August, and now—after the appearance of the cat—were only a half game out. They ended up winning 100 games—finished eight ahead of the Cubs. Went on to beat the Orioles four games to one in the World Series. No wonder they were dubbed the Amazin' Mets. You have to give them credit."

"I guess so," said a disgruntled Jason.

"But as I said before, no one can ever take away the memories of that long, hot summer. They were a great ball club, Leo's Cubs. Santo, Williams, Beckert, Kessinger, Hundley, Jenkins—they all played together for eight seasons. Banks for six of those before he retired. You don't see that today. I believe that's why they remained close friends after their careers ended. They had been soldiers together and only they could relate to what it was like in the trenches."

Although Abner could be a bit melodramatic at times, the boys liked his analogy. In 2020, baseball people remembered the 1969 Cubs in such a negative light. It was always America's darlings (the Amazin' Mets) versus those villains from Chicago (especially Leo). What should have been the Cubs' turn to win it all ended up being a story of failure and frustration. But, when it all came to pass, it made for a pretty good story. Like Abner said, a "great love affair" between a team and its fans.

Matt and Jason stood up.

"Well," said Matt, "we should be going. School tomorrow."

"Yep. Be sure to let me know your grade on the project."

"We will."

"Oh, and the next time you visit the ballpark, spend some time admiring those statues of Williams, Santo, and Banks. That kid—Lou Cella—did a great job on them."

CHAPTER 17

Whether Mrs. Peck actually wept when she read the boys' report was a matter of conjecture. What she wrote across the bottom of the title page was not: *Matt and Jason, your excellent essay on Mr. Tripplehorn's tragic loss was very touching. It is not often that I receive such sensitive writing from freshmen. I am proud of your work, as you should be.* Directly above her neat script sat—in all its big, bold glory—an A.

The talk in the faculty lounge centered on the grade and whether Mrs. Peck was going soft in her advancing years. When, they asked, had this grand matron ever given a superior mark to a novice writer? Never, that's when, was the general consensus among her peers. Her job was to mold the freshmen as the year rolled along into "average" writers, not to become slaphappy with the A's and B's right off the bat.

But, when questioned by her department head about the unusual evaluation, Mrs. Peck responded, "These boys did more than was expected. They didn't pen a quotidian report. They wrote about heartfelt pain, and in so doing, made transparent the man's soul for the reader to know. To achieve this, they didn't simply talk to the man. Any idiot could do that. Rather, they bonded with him in such an intimate way as to allow him to feel comfortable sharing this event, and its effect on his life, with them. I dare say these two might find employment as fine journalists someday."

And that was that.

Matt and Jason, not yet aware of Mrs. Peck's inordinately high standards for her students, were nonetheless thrilled with the grade. The project that had haunted their summer without a ghost of a chance to succeed had been transformed into the apex of the boys' academic careers. And they knew whom they had to thank.

"Should we bring it right over to show him?" asked Jason.

"Too early," said Matt. "Game's still on."

The Cubs were hosting the Marlins at Wrigley, and one of Abner's original admonitions had been to not bother him during games. As much as possible, the boys tried to adhere to this. "Besides," added Matt, "we have to stop home for his present."

Abner's "present" was the Ron Santo postcard he had requested when the boys were leaving for the Hall of Fame. In the excitement of the past week, they had forgotten to give it to him.

It was decided that they would wait until after dinner to visit. The only thing Abner hated more than being interrupted while watching his beloved Cubs was being kept from his regular meals.

The essay made the rounds of both houses during the late afternoon. Mrs. Doyle held it up for Mr. Doyle to see when he arrived home from his job as a real estate agent. "That's my boy," he said, grabbing Jason in a headlock and raining friendly noogies upon him.

"Cut it out, Dad!" Breaking away from his father, Jason asked if he could eat dinner at Matt's house and then go visit Abner.

"Is your homework done?"

"Yes," he lied.

"Then, yes, you may. But be home by nine."

Mr. and Mrs. Holmes were only a little more subdued. Mrs. Holmes was aware of her son's deficiencies in writing and was overjoyed with the grade and, especially, the teacher's comments. Secretly fearing a disastrous outcome on the essay, she had spent the afternoon preparing Matt's favorite comfort food—meatloaf and mashed potatoes—and the family and Jason were now feasting on the meal.

"You see what happens when you don't wait 'til the last minute to finish your work?" proclaimed Mr. Holmes, triggering furtive glances of guilt between the two boys. Apparently,

Matt's father had forgotten the scolding he had given his son on the trip to Gettysburg. "Yes, sir, when you get things done ahead of time, you get good results."

Or, sometimes, good things just happen.

****

"Congratulations!" exclaimed a beaming Abby. Matt and Jason presented to her the fruit of their work, the gold having finally been panned in the waning hours of summer. She read it over carefully, wiping a tear from her eye as she finished.

"Boys, this is beautifully written. You did a nice job. I'm sure Abner will be pleased."

"Is he in his room?" asked Matt.

"I don't know. The last I saw of him he was in the cafeteria downing his second piece of coconut cream pie. But he could be anywhere now."

"Here he comes," said Jason, pointing down the hall.

Abner ambled toward them, swinging his cane and whistling like Gene Kelly. His sudden fame was sitting well with him, especially around the home, where the ladies were paying even more attention to his antics than usual.

"Well, well, well, if it isn't Kukla, Fran, and Ollie. I didn't expect to see you fellows so soon. Weren't you just here yesterday?"

"Yes, they were here yesterday," answered Abby. "As you well remember."

Abner flashed an impish grin. "Why, of course I remember. And if Fran here will dismiss her little puppets, we'll adjourn to my quarters and talk."

"Have a nice time," said Abby as she headed back to her duties. "I'll see you all later."

Room 101 had become a familiar second home to the boys. They plopped comfortably on the bed next to Abner's. Jason put his head on the pillow and stretched out his legs.

"We have a gift for you," said Matt. "Two gifts actually."

"Can't beat that. What are they?"

Matt reached out and handed the postcard to Abner.

The old man grinned. "Why, I'd forgotten all about this. Thank you. Thank you very much."

"Here's the other one."

Abner took the essay and studied the title page. He read Mrs. Peck's comments twice. Carefully, he set it on his desk. "Is it all right if I read it after you've left?"

"Sure," answered Matt.

"Thanks. I'll return it the next time I see you. And allow me to add my congratulations to the mix. I'm also proud of you two."

Abner paused and picked up the desk phone. "Give me a minute, boys. Shirley, this is Abner. Is Abby still in the building? She is? Good. Tell her to bring the key around, will ya?"

Matt and Jason shot quizzical glances at each other.

Abner stood. "I need your help. We've got to find a spot for Ron. Do me a favor and look under my bed."

Matt and Jason did so. A huge black trunk greeted them. It took up every available inch of space beneath the bed.

"What's this?" asked Jason.

"You'll see. Pull it out."

The boys strained to slide the massive trunk from out of its hiding place. When they'd completed the task, it sat wedged between the two beds. Bordered in ornate gold, it spoke of vast treasures gathered over many years, the personal plunder of a forgotten pirate. Little did they realize . . .

Abby bounded into the room, a key ring with a solitary gold key visible in her hand. "Is this what you want, Long John?"

"Yes, I wish to show the lads my hoard," sneered Abner. "And don't speak disrespectfully of the aged."

She handed him the key and smiled at the boys. She said, "Have fun." Then, she gave Abner a knowing wink and hurried from the room.

Perplexed as usual, Matt and Jason waited for the veil to be lifted.

"Open it," Abner commanded, handing the key to Matt.

Matt inserted it into the lock and turned it over. Next, he threw open the clasp and, together with Jason, propped open the lid. Eyes open wide, they looked at Abner, who smiled like Santa on Christmas morning.

"Don't just sit there. Take a look-see."

"You mean we can touch it?"

"Of course. I trust you to handle with care."

Inside was a staggering array of everything baseball. Autographed photos and balls, scorecards and pennants, bobble-head dolls, and other vintage memorabilia from the game's illustrious history—none of it purchased secondhand. These were all Abner "originals."

"Pretty cool, eh?"

The boys' mouths were open, but no words came out.

For the next hour or so, Matt and Jason poured over Abner's "trinkets," as he called them, reliving the stories he had shared with them, and then some.

"You have Jackie Robinson's autograph?" asked a stunned Jason.

"You can see it for yourself. I assure you it's not a fake. When the Dodgers came to Wrigley for the first time in '47, all the colored folk came out to see him. After the game, I stood with them in the roped-off section and waited patiently for Jackie to come over and sign. Eventually, he did. I figured I should get the autograph of the most courageous man to ever play the game for my little collection. I'm glad I hung around for a spell that day. It was worth it. If you look carefully in there, you'll find autographs of Satchel Paige and Josh Gibson as well. Baseball, you see, was meant to be played by everyone, all the races on the same field. Works out better that way."

"This is amazing," said Matt, almost out of breath.

"Aren't you worried about somebody stealing this stuff?" asked Jason.

"Not really. First of all, none of the folks around here know of its existence, and Abs's got the only key. Second, the trunk's too heavy to be carted off, especially by the oldsters." Abner snickered at the thought of "Moonshine" Mulligan and another decrepit citizen of the home trying to steer the heavy trunk out the door to a waiting U-Haul. "Why, they'd split their spleens."

Matt and Jason laughed.

"Third, if they want it, they can have it. I can't take it where I'm going, you know."

This inevitable fact stung the boys.

"Finally, and most importantly, the only two items special to me are tucked away in a safe deposit box over at the bank."

"What—" began Jason.

"Don't ask. It seems to me you boys have enough to study over right in front of you."

It was true. A treasure–trove was spread out before them, and it would take weeks to sort through it. Outside of the Hall of Fame's collection, this might well have been the most unique of its kind.

"What's this?" asked Matt, holding up what looked like a child's glove.

"Ha!" barked Abner. "That's my first mitt. Don't you know that every red-blooded American male still has his first baseball glove? It's hidden away on some closet shelf or in a box in the garage. But it's there. It's a reminder of all that was good about his childhood, and he's not ready to let that go just yet. So, every now and then, when the house is still and no one's around, he takes it out of its secret place and puts it on. Then, he imagines his whole life is ahead of him. His friends are at the back door calling on him to come out and play. The summer sun is ever so hot, and the ball field is just down the block. How can he say no?"

Matt and Jason knew where their first gloves were tucked away. When each had received his new one, he somehow couldn't find it in his heart to toss the old one in the trash.

Outside, the sun had set. Inside, Abner's desk lamp cast shadows onto the wall. The boys wanted to stay all night, to sift through the sands of time set before them, one marvelous grain at a time.

"Can we come back sometime and look through all this?" asked Jason.

"Anytime you want. But it's almost nine o'clock, and 'CSI: Omaha' is coming on. So, I want you ruffians to skedaddle."

Abner turned on the TV.

Matt and Jason carefully placed a few items back in the trunk and shut the lid. Matt turned the key in the lock. Then, on their knees, they pushed the trunk back into its place beneath the bed.

Abner glanced at them over his shoulder. "Thank you, boys. Just leave the key with Abs on your way out. Pleasant dreams."

Matt and Jason ushered themselves quietly out of the room as the popular theme song for CBS' hit drama blared from the Bose speakers beside the TV. Abner sang along. He had become a fan of the Who at the ripe old age of sixty-seven. He liked their stage presence.

CHAPTER 18

If CUBS was an acronym, what would it stand for? That's an easy one, sports fans. Over the years, disgruntled followers of the team coined the phrase "Completely Useless By September" as a way of mocking the ball club's slim chances of clinching a pennant or division title. However, 2020 was different. By mid-September, about the time Abner left for Los Angeles—escorted by Abby on this trip—the Cubs had pulled to within a game of St. Louis after a three-game sweep of the Reds in Cincinnati while the Cardinals were dropping three in a row at home to the Phillies. The next night, an off-day for the Cubs, the Cardinals lost again, this time to the Pirates. The Cubs were only a half game out of first.

The club was clicking on all cylinders. Banks led the N.L. with 40 home runs and 123 RBIs. Castro was hitting .360 and had swiped 82 bases, including home twice. And the pitchers had notched their fair share of wins: Wood was 18-8; Jenkins, 18-10; and Brown 16-5. Pennant fever gripped the North Side.

Just before Abner boarded his flight, he phoned Matt to tell him and Jason to "get the Cubs over the hump" while he was gone. His parting words were: "And don't take any wooden nickels." Matt promised he wouldn't, although he had no idea what Abner meant by the archaic saying.

The old man, with all the moxie he could muster, took L.A. by storm. "The Tonight Show" claimed its biggest rating since Tiny Tim wed Miss Vicki at the end of the sixties. Host Chris Rock was moved to tears of laughter as his guest told one hilarious yarn after another. To cap the show, Abner joined the band and warbled a delightfully off-key rendition of "Sentimental Journey." The studio audience went bonkers.

The following Monday, Alex Trebek welcomed America's favorite senior to a taping of "Jeopardy!" (After a series of hosts had failed to fill Alex's shoes following the popular host's retirement several years earlier, ABC begged him to return to his familiar role to start the new season.) Abner held his own against the returning champion, a first-grade teacher from Connersville, Indiana, and another challenger, a lineman from Wichita, Kansas. It was a close game that ultimately came down to Final Jeopardy. When the category came up Baseball, Abner just smiled. He knew it would be a walk-off.

"This U.S. president became the first to throw out the game ball on opening day," intoned Alex.

The first-grade teacher, who had never watched a baseball game in her life, guessed George Washington.

The Wichita lineman went with Kansas' favorite son, Dwight D. Eisenhower.

Both were incorrect, the teacher by over a century.

Abner, of course, knew that William Howard Taft had opened the Washington Senators' 1910 season by throwing out the ceremonial game ball from his box seat in National Park. No other U.S. president had done so before.

"Who is Taft? That is correct! Let's see how much you risked . . . $16,400—all of it! That's $32,800, and it makes you our new champion!"

Abner wasn't finished. He flexed his mental muscles over the next four days, sweeping the week and earning a five-day total of $185,200, all of which he promptly donated to a local veterans' charity. At his age, money held no special allure. It did, however, have a way of making mad "Moonshine" Mulligan, who had made the trip with Abner and Abby, and who was not pleased with the old man's sudden generosity.

With Abner's West Coast stay extended, Hollywood came calling. Warner Brothers studio was planning a sequel to *The Lord of the Rings* trilogy and wanted him to play Gandalf. There was also talk of remaking the 1946 classic *It's a Wonderful Life* with Abner in the role of the peevish Mr. Potter. "Moonshine" was drooling over these unforeseen opportunities, but Abner turned down all the offers, insisting that he wasn't cut out to be someone else; he was just happy being himself. Abby agreed, although she commented that portraying the constantly crabby Potter wouldn't require much acting on Abner's part. In turn, he facetiously threatened to send her home early, back to Chicago, where the Cubs just couldn't seem to get past the Cardinals.

Ironically—or perhaps appropriately—the day they finally vaulted over St. Louis into first place was a gorgeous, sunny Sunday at Dodger Stadium in Chavez Ravine. And Abner Doubleday Tripplehorn was there to throw out the ceremonial game ball, just as President Taft had done over a century earlier.

The pre-game festivities began with a photo shoot at home plate where Abner—wearing his Cubs cap—posed with Dodger players. Then, using his cane for balance, he climbed slowly up the pitcher's mound. There, standing on the bump where Koufax and Drysdale had once intimidated even the best N.L. hitters, the old man lobbed the ball into the catcher, a rookie just up from the minors. It bounced once before reaching its destination. Even a last-minute surge of adrenaline had not permitted Abner to throw the ball the entire distance on the fly. But, right now, that didn't matter. 56,000 fans stood as one and roared their approval. In the box seats behind home plate, Abby wiped away a grateful tear. "Moonshine," still grieving over the loss of his client's movie-star income, choked down one Dodger Dog after another.

Walking off the mound onto the neatly manicured grass, Abner doffed his cap to the crowd. It was just the beginning of a glorious day.

In the fifth inning, with the Cubs trailing 3-0, a final score was posted from Milwaukee. The Brewers had bested the Cardinals 2-1. The Cubs were tied for first place in the National League Central Division. If they could only come from behind to win the game. If they could only score some runs.

They did. They plated sixteen of them, including nine in the sixth inning, to crush the Dodgers and take over sole possession of first place.

"Time to go home," said Abner to Abby when the last out was recorded. "This may well be my last pennant race, and I don't wanna miss it."

"Moonshine" objected. He thought Abner was being too hasty. "After all," the greedy agent pleaded, "there's more money to be made."

"Not for you. You're fired. Abs, be a gem and call Mr. Trebek for me. Tell him to give my spot on the show to someone else. I'm going home." Abner turned to face his ex-agent. "One more thing. You owe me for the hot dogs."

****

Most pennant races are thrilling, heart-stopping roller coaster rides where one day a team comes from behind in improbable fashion while its rival blows one in the ninth, and the next day, in a stunning reversal of fortune, some ill-fated player gets picked off base or drops an easy fly ball to lose the game while the rival celebrates a walk-off win. Such is the nature of September—or in this case, October—baseball.

When the 2020 Cubs finally clinched their division on the last weekend of the season by beating the Pirates at home while the Cardinals were losing in Atlanta, their fans let out an exhausted sigh of relief along with the delirious cheers.

But the party didn't last long. The playoffs, as treacherous as a bog after rain, loomed ahead. All throughout Chicagoland, prescriptions for Xanax were refilled, and drug stores sold out their supplies of Maalox. Everybody except kids and teens took a wait-and-see attitude, having been burned so often in the past.

Too young to remember 2008, the last time the Cubs had qualified for the post-season, Matt and Jason took an optimistic view. They joined Abner at the home to watch the Padres upset the Phillies in a one-game wild-card match. Two days hence, the Cubs would host the Padres for the start of the five-game National League Division Series. (The other NLDS would feature the Marlins against the Giants.)

"The Padres," stated Jason with contempt. "Who would've thunk it? The Cubs shouldn't have any trouble beating them."

"Hmmm," said Abner. "That's not the first time I've heard that."

"What d'ya mean?"

"I know what he means," chimed in Matt. "1984, right?"

"Correct," said Abner.

"That's when the Cubs got screwed because they didn't have lights at Wrigley Field. So, they had to play the last three games in San Diego and wound up losing them all."

"Incorrect."

"Huh?"

"I repeat. Incorrect. Oh, they lost all three in San Diego all right. But they did *not* lose their home-field advantage because of Wrigley's lack of lights. That, my lads, is one of the biggest myths in Chicago sports history."

The boys sat silently, aware that Abner was about to set them straight. No need to argue.

"Starting in 1969—that's when the leagues broke into two divisions each, East and West—they alternated sites for what was then the only playoffs before the World Series. Five games. The first two were played in the N.L. East's home park in even-numbered years, with the last three hosted by the N.L. West team. 1984—an even-numbered year, right? First two games in Chicago, last three in San Diego. That's exactly the way it went down. In spite of the ruckus after the Cubs lost that series, nothing had been rearranged. The confusion came about because MLB announced that, *if* the Cubs were to make it to the World Series, they would have to play Games 1, 2, 6, and 7 in the city of the American League Champions—Detroit as it turned out. Those were scheduled to be weekday games, and the network wanted those to be *night* games, which couldn't happen at Wrigley. Thus, the perception that the Cubs had been cheated."

"Then why did everyone believe the Cubs had given up a home game to the Padres?" asked Jason.

"Simple. The three-game sweep in San Diego after being up two games to none was a bitter pill to swallow for the fans. It was a convenient—if untrue—excuse for the failure of a team they had come to love." Abner paused and sighed deeply. "That one really hurt, boys. The Cubs had hammered everybody that year and were on their way to their first World Series appearance in thirty-nine years—a rematch of the '45 series against the Tigers. Ryne Sandberg was the N.L. MVP; Rick Sutcliffe won the Cy Young Award with a 16-1 record; Jim Frey was named Manager of the Year; Dallas Green was Executive of the Year. After winning the first two games at Wrigley 13-0 and 4-2, it was their destiny to win it all. And then the bottom fell out."

"What happened?" asked Jason.

"Well, they lost Game 3 by a score of 7-1. Game 4 was won by the Padres 7-5 on a walk-off homer. And then there was Sunday's game. Sutcliffe on the mound leading 3-2 in the bottom of the seventh with a runner in scoring position. Ground ball hit right to the first baseman. When it went through his legs, no one could believe it. Still can't. Score was tied. A barrage of hits followed and, three more runs later, the Padres led 6-3. That turned out to be the final score.

"Funny thing was, that first baseman had walloped a two-run homer in the top of the first. Mighty big hit if the Cubs had held the lead. He would have been one of the heroes instead of the goat. Baseball's cruel that way.

"Sick joke went around Chicago the next week that he was so depressed he jumped in front of a speeding El train. (Pause.) But don't worry. He wasn't hurt. The train went right through his legs."

"Well?" asked Matt.

"Well what?"

"Aren't you going to tell us the first baseman's name?"

Abner winced. "To tell the truth, it's too hard for me to say out loud."

"Kinda like the name that is beneath all names?" asked Jason.

"Something like that."

Recounting Cubs history wasn't often fun, and Abner looked worn and pale. The boys guessed that a small piece of Abner's heart had been removed that day in 1984.

"It rained that afternoon in Chicago," concluded Abner.

"We'll win it this year," said Jason. "You wait and see."

"That's right," echoed Matt. "Revenge on the Padres."

Abner laughed, buoyed by the spirit of youth suddenly alive in the small room. "Okay, boys. Whatever you say. We'll get 'em this time. I suppose that's what I'm hanging around to see."

CHAPTER 19

The Cubs' brass felt that the Dodgers had upstaged them. After all, Abner was *their* one-hundred-twenty-year-old icon. What was he doing gallivanting all over Los Angeles anyway? Consequently, they made sure he was booked to throw out the first pitch of the playoffs from Wrigley's mound.

The rush of excitement that cool fall evening could not be contained. The crowd, more boisterous than usual, made its way through the turnstiles a good two hours before the first pitch was scheduled. Many fans fueled their tanks with one $9.75 beer after another. Predictable signs such as THIS IS THE YEAR! and REVENGE FOR '84! were displayed from the bleachers to the far reaches of the upper deck. No one had expected these "new" Cubs to be in the post-season after the disappearance of the plane in March. No one had expected these young kids with familiar surnames to have a shot at the title that had eluded the club since 1908. Was it possible? Could this really, actually, finally be happening?

Once again, Abby, Matt, and Jason were Abner's guests, this time in seats behind the home dugout. When Abner shuffled out to the mound, it was announced that he had been eight years old the last time the Cubs were World Champions. The crowd exploded. More than a century of starvation was about to be fed. The old man was surely a talisman from the past. The fans would ride his tattered coattails to the Promised Land. True, it was a tall order for this modern-day Moses, but Abner somehow felt up to the task.

So did Brown, whose knuckler baffled the Padres all night. "Shorty" Wilson's two-run homer in the fourth held up, and the Cubs won 2-0. When the Cubs won the second game 5-2 behind

"Jolly" Jenkins, all of Chicago was as electrified as the El's infamous third rail.

The plane ride to San Diego was a calm, business-like one for the players. There was on board a modest level of self-assurance that suggested the trip back to Chicago in a few days would *not* be for Game 5. It would be over by then. But the farce of Games 3 and 4 gave notice to Cub Nation that the baseball gods were not yet through toying with their team. Both Wood and Holtzman were slapped around like Larry and Curly, inspiring one clever San Diego sportswriter to declare that the Padres suddenly had the "Moe"-mentum in the series.

"Meet me and Abs at the main gate," were Abner's instructions. Thus, the group was in the first-base box seats when "bizarro" history repeated itself.

When the young San Diego first baseman put the Padres ahead 2-1 with a solo shot onto Sheffield in the sixth, it might have behooved him to remember the oldest true saying in the world of baseball: "The game is never over until the last man is out." Instead, he basked greedily in the glory of the moment— *his* moment—happily accepting the backslaps and high-fives of his teammates in the dugout.

And when the ball was hit on the ground right toward him in the bottom of the ninth inning with runners on second and third and two outs, he "knew" the game was over. (Even though it wasn't.) As he bent down for the ball—as he had done thousands upon thousands of times since his days back in Little League—he let his mind flash ahead to the wild celebration that would take place in a moment. Jumping-shouting-happy tumbling amidst grown men in the middle of a green-mown infield. And then, as the crowd went suddenly silent—subdued by the inevitable—he closed his glove around the ball. Only the ball wasn't there. It had rocketed through his legs into right field. The fans erupted as the tying and winning runs scampered home. Now, it was over.

The party in Wrigleyville lasted until dawn, the usual suspects finally collared by overzealous cops who just wanted to go home to their families.

At Serenity Now the next day, Abner expressed a mixture of confidence and caution as he spoke with Matt and Jason on what had become their daily afternoon stroll.

"Yes, I think the Cubs can handle the Marlins. Assuming they don't get rerouted through the Bermuda Triangle to get to the games in Miami."

The boys chuckled at Abner's bad joke.

"Remember though," warned Abner, "they're a good team too. They wouldn't have won as many games if they weren't."

"Yeah, but the Cubs won more," Jason reminded Abner.

It was a gorgeous late October day. Resplendent in their overcoats of yellow, orange, and red, the leaves hung proudly on the trees. A slight breeze rushed past the dying foliage, sending a shower of the weaker ones cascading toward earth.

Abner reached out and snatched a rust-colored leaf from mid-air. He held it up for his friends to see, and it crumpled in his hand. "That's the way to go, boys. One second you're there, the next—poof. That's how I want to go when my time comes."

Matt and Jason were taken aback. This wasn't the first time Abner had commented on his own mortality, but it made them feel threatened, as if his passing would leave a void in their own lives that couldn't possibly be filled. Who, for instance, would they ever meet who had been a die-hard fan of the Chicago Whales? And who would ever again fill in their knowledge gaps when it came to baseball history? And who seemed always welcoming whenever they stopped by the home to visit?

"So, Abner," asked Matt, changing the subject, "my dad told me the Cubs were only five outs away from the World Series in 2003 when they played the Marlins in the NLCS. Is that true?"

"It is."

"And then some fan interfered or something?"

"More or less."

For the next half a block, no one spoke. The autumn leaves continued to fall. Matt and Jason supposed that Abner was deciding—as he had that first day they'd met and he'd asked them if they knew about Fred Merkle—whether it was worth it to go on.

"Steve Bartman."

"Huh?"

"That's who you want me to tell you about. Steve Bartman. The fan who interfered."

"Yeah," said a suddenly alert Jason, "I've heard that name before."

"I'm not surprised," said Abner. "The young man was vilified more than Capone in his heyday. You know, I'm not sure I could have stood up to the kind of abuse he took. And he took it all in the classiest possible way."

"What did he do?" asked Matt.

"Only what every single fan in the ballpark would have done if they'd been sitting where he was. What every fan in every ballpark in America does every night. He tried to catch a ball in the stands for a souvenir.

"Usually, it's the players who have their lives ruined by an occurrence during a game. Bill Buckner, for example. Tough-as-nails player who respected the game. Great hitter. He made one crucial error in a World Series game and was severely castigated by the fans, the media, everyone. Could never live it down. Predictable, I suppose. But a fan? I'm pretty sure there's never been another event like it in the history of the game. One thing, his fault or not, it altered reality that night, turned the mood of the crowd completely around."

"Well?" prodded an impatient Jason.

Abner sighed. This was one he didn't want to tell. "Okay. Game 6. Cubs up in the series, three games to two. Top of the eighth. Cubs ahead 3-0. Mark Prior, their ace, on the mound. One on, one out for the Marlins. The ball was hit into the left-field corner. As it fell to earth in foul territory, just beyond the wall, Cubs left fielder Moises Alou leapt up and stretched out to catch it. Bartman reached up and deflected it a millisecond before it landed in Alou's glove. Looking back, it might have been ruled interference, in which case the batter would have been out. It wasn't. Alou threw a fit. Shortly thereafter, Alex Gonzales, who led the National League in fielding percentage among shortstops that season, booted a routine double-play ball.

The Marlins scored eight runs. The next night, they came out higher than a kite and took Game 7. And the curse of the goat became the curse of Bartman."

"And you don't think he was responsible for the loss?" asked Jason.

Abner glared at the boy. "I don't chew my cabbage twice. I already said he was just doing what any normal fan would do. It certainly wasn't him that gave up the eight runs, was it? But he shouldered the blame. Hostile fans showered him with beer, threw hot dogs and pizza slices at him, cursed him, and even threatened to kill him. It was mob mentality at its worst. The poor fellow went into hiding the next day. With all of Cub Nation hunting for him as if he was John Wilkes Booth. A sorry spectacle for civilized people to behave that way. It would only be justice if, even now, he could be paid back in some way."

The rest of the walk was quiet. Matt and Jason spent the time reflecting on Abner's story. If baseball didn't always mirror the uncertainty of life, this game certainly had—for the players, the fans, and especially one heartbroken young man who never guessed how a trip to the ballpark would turn out for him.

****

By the time Game 7 of the National League Championship Series was to be played, it was well into November. Fortunately, an Indian summer had produced a spell of warm weather, and the fans were decked out in sweatshirts and light jackets. This was it. For the first time in seventeen long years—since the debacle of 2003—the Cubs were one win away from playing in the World Series. Their old rivals, the Tigers, awaited them, having beaten the Yankees in their own Game 7 for the American League crown.

The Goodyear Blimp hovered lazily over the hungry crowd. Its camera zoomed down onto the right-field bleachers. In the first row sat Abner, Abby, Matt, and Jason. Unbeknownst to the others, Abner had been offered choice box seats once again but had turned them down. He had asked for these seats specifically to recall his viewpoint during Game 6 of the 1945 World Series. By now, the boys understood the significance of *that* game in Abner's life.

The pre-game hoopla ended with a drunken fan streaking across the outfield. The other drunken fans hooted and hollered their approval and booed the security guards who dragged the young rowdy off to his awaiting escort of CPD officers.

"Just think what he'll be missing tonight," stated Abner. "A Cub pennant. I don't think they have TVs in the Cook County holding cells."

The boys laughed not so much at the joke but at Abner's optimism about the outcome of the game. And why not? After all, if this man, who had absorbed more Cubs wins and losses than anyone in history, could gaze down on the assembled troops—standing at attention for the National Anthem—with pride and enthusiasm, then they could too.

Surely, if Abner Doubleday Tripplehorn felt upbeat about their chances, then everyone should feel upbeat: everyone inside the park, on the streets and sidewalks, on bike paths and El trains, in their apartments and condos, the young, the old, the infirmed, Democrats, Republicans, Independents—everyone.

The game itself was all the network had hoped for: a topsy-turvy, rumble-in-the-jungle, down-and-dirty affair. Men were struck with pitched balls, picked off base, thrown out at home, and left stranded on third. Infielders saved pitchers with highlight-reel double plays, and outfielders sprinted over acres of mown grass to spear hard-hit balls in the gaps. Catchers blocked potential wild pitches with their already bruised bodies, and umpires felt the fiery wrath of crazed fans and bench jockeys on every close call. Up and down. Back and forth.

During the heated battle, when he wasn't recording the action in his scorecard, Abner chatted amiably with the middle-aged man seated next to him. The stranger wore a green turtleneck under a black sweatshirt; a Cubs cap was perched on his head. He politely removed his earphones—through which he listened intently to the broadcast of the game—whenever Abner spoke to him.

By the top of the ninth inning, the exhausted fans had ascended Mt. Everest, only to be caught in an avalanche and somersaulted back to the bottom of the mighty peak. The Cubs had grabbed their third lead of the night in the seventh. But a two-run homer in the ninth off the normally reliable "Sober" Sutter had tied the game at nine apiece. The world was caving in.

Fearful fans were beside themselves with angst. Why hadn't "Sober" reeled in the fish? Were their heroes going to tank once again?

Tension froze the faithful in their seats as "Stretch" Williams came to bat to lead off the bottom of the ninth. Only "Boom-Boom" Banks had hit more home runs (49) during the season than Williams (45). Could he, like the legendary Roy Hobbs, win it with a blow?

Veteran announcer Jack Brickhead leaned into his microphone, a cigar stub clenched between his teeth. "Oh, brother. This is really something. I don't think it's an understatement to say that this is the biggest at-bat of the season for Williams. Oh, brother."

The first pitch from the Marlins lefty was a curve that broke low and outside. "Stretch" didn't budge.

"Oh, man. I'm surprised he didn't start Williams with a fastball to try and get ahead in the count. You have to give the slugger credit for laying off that one."

The next one *was* a fastball—right down Broadway.

Williams didn't miss it.

"There's a high drive to right! Back . . . back . . . back . . ."

The announcer's famous home-run call crackled over the airwaves as the ball descended rapidly toward the first row of the bleachers.

It was headed directly toward Abner. The old man struggled to react in time, to get his hands up to protect his face. But he couldn't quite make it. An instant before the baseball crashed into his forehead, the stranger beside him reached out and, in a sure-handed grab, clutched the ball firmly. It wasn't just any ball either. It was the home-run ball that won the Cubs their first

National League pennant since 1945. And it would make the stranger a very rich man in the days to come.

Before Abner could thank his new friend for saving him from a severe concussion that easily could have ended the old man's life, the stranger disappeared into the delirious crowd and headed home to the life of solitude he preferred.

CHAPTER 20

It was a gorgeous day for baseball. That's right. Day. Commissioner Bush had declared that this bright, beautiful Sunday before Thanksgiving was the perfect afternoon to play Game 7 of the 2020 World Series. No longer would bleary-eyed adults struggle into work the day after a fourteen-inning marathon that ended at 3:30 am ET. No longer would school-aged children sit up past midnight to watch the final out of the season. It was baseball in daylight, the way the game was supposed to be played.

The first six games had stressed the home-field advantage. Games 1, 2, and 6 were taken by the Cubs in Chicago. The middle three belonged to the Tigers in Detroit. Television ratings were at an all-time high, presumably because the entire nation wanted to see whether the Cubs would at long last end the horrible curse that hung over them. A circus atmosphere permeated the streets of Chicago's North Side—like Christmas and the Fourth of July all wrapped up in one zany package. Who would've thunk it?

But all was not positive thought. The city's most dogged rumor revolved around the unexpected arrival of the original 2020 Cubs, their plane having been abducted by aliens and returned in time for the team to claim its "rightful" place in the World Series. "Ozzie sightings" were everywhere, as common as Bigfoot and Loch Ness, and every bit as frightful too. Fans could see the volatile Venezuelan demanding an opportunity to manage *his* Cubs once again, claiming that the "new" Cubs were just replacement players. A lawsuit might halt the games until the conundrum could be worked out to everyone's satisfaction, which meant Game 7 might not be played until mid-December. (Sort of like the NHL and NBA Finals being played in June.)

But all this madness was to be expected. The Chicago Cubs, after all, had last played in a World Series a few months after Hiroshima, and loyal fans had to let off some steam to relieve their tension. In general, there was a "haven't-gone-into-work-all-week-and-haven't-even-bothered-to-call-in-sick" attitude that had a grip on the city's working stiffs. Oh, yeah, beer sales were also up all over town.

President Hillary Clinton arrived in Air Force One at 7:15 am. A consummate politician, she had reversed her Yankee-fan status from her years as a New York senator to reclaim her original "I grew up as a Cubs fan in the northwest suburbs" position. Consequently, she was invited by the Ricketts family to attend a before-the-game brunch at Harry Caray's. Other invitees included former players, the Rahmfather, and, of course, Abner Doubleday Tripplehorn and his traveling companion Abby.

A splendid time was guaranteed for all.

Steve Goodman's classic song "Go Cubs Go!" and the even older "Hey! Hey! Holy Mackerel!" blared from speakers during the festivities. King Theo greeted the assemblage and spoke optimistically about the culmination of his decade-long project to build the Cubs into a championship-caliber team. And the food was scrumptious. The favorite was the goat and mushroom casserole.

Speaking of goats, there was a citywide ban on any type of sacrificial mutilation of the animals, sparked by the desire to appease all goats everywhere so they wouldn't be tempted to arise as one and crush all hope. In fact, part of the opening ceremonies at Game 1 had included members of the Sianis' family being allowed to bring a direct descendent of old Billy's goat into Wrigley Field for a "Blessing of the Goat" rite. The goat responded favorably, marking his territory by peeing on home plate, and the Cubs went out and won the first two games.

So, when a taxi dropped Abner and Abby off at the corner of Clark and Addison, there was a certain magic in the air. For Abner, this was a culmination of sorts as well. He had never guessed, as he stood waiting in this same spot for his twenty-two-year-old son to arrive before Game 7 in 1945, that he would have to wait so long for another chance to see his Cubs play for all the marbles. All seemed right with the world again as it had on that fateful day so many years ago. The only difference, it seemed to him, was that now he was waiting for two boys, his new friends Matt and Jason. He cast his eyes down the block toward where they would be coming in from the El with the rest of the crowd.

And, so it was that, like a time traveler, Abner found himself back in 1945. The colorful clothes on the people surrounding him were replaced with the brown overcoats and gray fedoras of the day. Men milled around the entrance, waiting for the gates to open. (Only a few women and hardly any children were present.) He knew, as he stood holding two tickets for the right-field bleachers—where he and Francis had sat two days earlier for the Cubs' twelfth-inning victory—that he was a wealthy man. He and his wife Vera had been blessed with good health, good jobs, and most of all, a wonderful son. A son who, unlike some of their less fortunate neighbors and co-workers, had come home alive and uninjured from the horrors of World War II. A son who had a steady job with the United States Post Office and who was preparing to ask a certain young girl to marry him. A son who . . .

Abner was confused. Suddenly, he didn't feel well at all. Who, again, was he waiting for? And why was the impending arrival causing him so much consternation? Wasn't this a happy occasion?

He felt someone grab his arm. He turned to see a woman he didn't recognize. She was saying something and pointing down the block.

"Here he comes! We won't miss the first pitch!" Abner yelled.

Abby, who could see both Matt and Jason clearly, wondered why Abner referred to the two boys as "he."

And then Abner saw clearly as well. And what he saw terrified him. He could see Francis smiling and waving and breaking into a jog, picking up speed as he neared the intersection. And, because this event had been stored in his memory for seventy-five long years, he also saw what would happen next. The car swerving as it made the sharp turn; the screeching of the brakes; the sickening thud; his only son thrown to the pavement.

"Francis, no!" he yelled. "Stop!"

Abner broke from Abby's firm grip and lunged forward. He took two or three halting steps and collapsed on the ground, clutching at his chest as he fell.

Abby dropped to her knees to aid him. It was too late.

Matt and Jason approached in time to see the crestfallen nurse weeping over Abner. In many ways, it was the saddest day of their lives.

****

As soon as Abner's body was removed, Abby spoke to the boys. "I'm going back to the home and start planning the funeral. But there's absolutely no reason why you two can't go in and watch the game. Obviously, there's nothing you can do for him now, and somehow, I suspect he would have wanted you to cheer the Cubs on in his place. In fact, I'm sure of it."

Matt wiped a tear from his eye. "We can't do that."

"The last thing in the world either one of us wants to do is watch a baseball game," Jason added.

"It may seem that way at the moment. But do it for Abner. As a way of honoring him. Besides, I'm sure he and Vera and Francis are all going to enjoy the game together." She smiled and pointed skyward. "Best seats in the house."

And so, Matthew Holmes and Jason Doyle sat in the right-field bleachers in the same seats where Abner Doubleday Tripplehorn and his son Francis had sat during Game 6 of the 1945 World Series. Knowing of the old man's love of food, they downed a couple of hot dogs and Frosty Malts in his honor. They cried a little and laughed a lot, good proportions for the game of life.

And, oh yes, "Boom-Boom" Banks hit a grand-slam home run with two outs in the bottom of the ninth inning to win the game 4-3. For the first time since 1908, The Chicago National League Ball Club—otherwise known as the Cubs—were World Champions!

EPILOGUE

Sometime after Abner was laid to rest, a few of his closest friends were summoned to a reading of his will. In spite of his recent fame, the old fellow didn't have a ton of money. And what there was went to various charities. But there *was* the baseball memorabilia. However, as might be expected from someone so in love with the history of baseball, Abner willed the trunk's entire contents to the Baseball Hall of Fame in Cooperstown, New York.

That left only two other items of note: one sentimental, the other not so much—although it was much older. (Abner had once mentioned to Matt and Jason that these had been secured in a safe deposit box.) The oldest item was willed to Abby with the request—no, the command—from Abner that she sell it for all it was worth. As it turned out, it was worth a whole bunch—$2.9 million to be exact. It was a T206-card of Honus Wagner (vintage 1909), the rarest baseball card in the world. From now on, Abby wouldn't have to count on her meager savings to keep her afloat as she approached her own senior years. "Justice," Abner would have called it, for the lady who, after Vera, had been most dear to him in his life.

The other item, which was willed to Matt and Jason, was the single most significant memento in Abner's entire life. He knew, somehow, that it was in safe hands, that it would be treasured as he had treasured it. That the boys would look at it often and think of an old friend, one who had come into their lives when they most needed a fresh perspective. It was a program from the 1945 World Series. The Game 6 victory had been neatly scored in Abner's familiar script. At the bottom of the front cover was the date: October 8th. Beneath that he had scrawled the words: "With Francis."

****

The missing plane was never found. Legend has it that aliens did, indeed, capture it and haul its passengers away to some remote corner of the galaxy. One member of the squad was too unruly, however, and was supposedly dumped back into the jungle of a remote island somewhere in Caribbean waters. To this day, it's rumored that the poor guy still lives there—but not alone. He and another fellow about eighty-five sit by the campfire night after night playing guitars and singing songs. Their favorite number is "Are You Lonesome Tonight?" The little guy insists they sing it in Spanish.

Review Requested:
If you loved this book, would you please provide a review at Amazon.com?

CPSIA information can be obtained
at www.ICGtesting.com
Printed in the USA
BVHW031423050919
557660BV00005B/84/P

9 781950 860401